UNDER THE MIDNIGHT SUN

THE ADVENTURES OF DALTON LAIRD

BOOK TWO

A NOVEL BY
RUSSELL M. CHACE

TUKONA BOOKS LLC
P.O. Box 447; Cañon City, CO 81215

FOR MORE INFORMATION, CONTACT:
TUKONA BOOKS

P.O. BOX 447, CANON CITY, COLORADO 81215

TRADE PAPERBACK ISBN: 978-1-733037-12-9

E-BOOK ISBN: 978-1-733037-13-6

LIBRARY OF CONGRESS CONTROL NUMBER: APPLIED FOR

PRINTED IN THE UNITED STATES.

10 9 8 7 6 5 4 3 2

FIRST EDITION: DECEMBER 2018

To my sons, Matthew and Owen,

May you always draw closer to Him,

as you enjoy your time alone in God's great creation.

PROLOGUE

FOR MONTHS ON END, THE interior of Alaska is locked tight in the grip of winter. Her ermine white robe of snow lies thick on the taiga and tundra with a silence you can almost hear. Under this robe, in the rivulets and rivers, sheltered from the extreme cold, water gurgles and dances along in a relentless search for the Bering Sea, sometimes forced through cracks in the ice to run along just under the snow, sometimes below the ice. But always searching... searching.

Steadily, sunlight lengthens, the warm chinook winds blow, and within a couple of weeks, it seems, the forces of summer has broken winter's grip. Break-up, it is called.

The ermine white robe turns to slush that drips, trickles, gurgles, splashes and leaps to the rivers, then roars and rips the death-like grip of the ice from its banks. Defeated, the ice rises, breaks apart to boulder size chunks, and starts to move, relentlessly pushing and shoving ahead, grinding and crushing everything in its path. The rivers are cleansed of driftwood and the flotsam of human refuse left behind.

Ice dams form, backing up water, flooding low-lying areas, providing perfect breeding grounds for billions of mosquitoes, hungry for a blood meal. Some years are worse than others. Such was the spring of 1912 when two mangled prospectors' bodies were found floating in the ice and debris of the Chatanika River.

CHAPTER 1

I SAT IN FRONT OF THE desk wondering what this was all about. US Marshal Harvey P. Sullivan stood on the other side shuffling some papers. I had a suspicion the new Marshal wanted me to do some kind of work for him and I was determined to turn him down. I was through with law enforcement. Besides, I had a new bride waiting for me at home.

The frame building smelled musty and dank from the floodwaters that had finally receded back into the banks of the Chena River a couple of weeks earlier. Looking around the room, it did not seem like it had sustained much damage, other than the wallpaper curling up from the bottom edge. In the corner, an electric fan oscillated, keeping the air in constant movement, and the windows were open for fresh air. On the wood stove rested a pie tin containing a piece of smoldering Chaga fungus, used to keep mosquitoes at bay.

"Sorry for the mess," he said.

I looked back at the Marshal.

"I just got most of this paperwork dried out," he continued, "and now I'm trying to get it all filed away. From what I hear, that was the worst spring flood Fairbanks has had since E.T. Barnett landed here ten years ago, in 1901."

"Yeah, it was a good one alright. Mind tellin' me what this is about? Your telegram didn't give much information," I said.

The Marshal stopped moving with a hand full of papers and then looked down at me for the first time since I came in here. A sort of smile crossed his face.

"Dreibelbis was right. You don't like to waste time. Get right down to it, so to speak."

"Anything wrong with that?" I asked.

"No. No, none at all," he said with a smile and shaking his head.

Marshal Sullivan sat down, rested both elbows on the arms of his chair, touched the fingertips of both hands together, and stared at me for about two seconds. Then he said with a serious tone, "Dalton, I need your help."

'*Now what?*' I wondered.

"Let me summarize briefly. I just took over this assignment not too long ago. You know that; heck, everyone knows that. But from what I can ascertain from the reports is that, since the capture of the Blue Parka Man five years ago, back in '06, things in Fairbanks have been relatively mild. Then, all of a sudden, last fall, thanks to you, three Indian murders were solved and the Interior Syndicate was shut down."

Silence filled the room as Sullivan stared off into space, apparently lost in thought.

"Okay," I said. "And you're welcome, by the way. But what's your point?"

Sullivan frowned, looked back at me, leaned forward, and placed both arms on his desk.

"There's more," he said. "Since breakup, two bodies have floated down the Chatanika."

'*Finding bodies in the rivers during and after breakup happens sometimes*,' I thought to myself.

"Well, sir," I began, "I know you're new to Alaska and all, but that's not all that unusual. Many men have made mistakes crossing rotten ice, or got caught in a flood when the ice goes out and drown or whatever." I hoped I had not insulted his intelligence.

The Marshal briefly smiled then leaned back and said, "I know, we've had a few of them as well. But these two had a bullet hole in the head and teeth freshly dug out of their jaws. They were known to have had gold fillings in their teeth. Last fall, a dead miner was found on his claim on the Chatanika. He, too, had been shot and some of his teeth had been pried out of his jaw."

I smiled.

"Somethin' funny?"

"No, sir. I was just thinkin' that that's a new one on me. Evidently, somebody has staked a claim on dental work."

Sullivan frowned. Evidently, he didn't like my sense of humor. He got up, walked to the wood stove, picked up the coffee pot, and poured himself a cup. Then he held it out to me as if asking if I wanted any. I shook my head 'no'. It was probably old and strong anyway.

"So, where do I come in?" I asked as he walked back to his chair.

Sullivan sat down, took a sip of coffee, sat the cup down and said, "One of my deputies did the preliminary investigation. He couldn't come up with anything. All the miners in Chatanika are tight-lipped. I think they are all scared, suspecting each other. There's been a few fistfights, but no gun-play, yet. You have a good reputation with the miners and trappers here. They trust you. I don't believe they will see you as one of my deputies. I think you may be able to get some information on who may be the culprit, track him down to where ever he's hiding, and bring him in."

Man tracking and fugitive apprehension.

The last time I did any of that…well, I didn't want to think about it.

"Um…no. I'll pass on this one." I said.

The marshal's gaze met mine. His eyes narrowed a bit. "Dalton I need you on this. Dreibelbis has told me you're the best tracker he knows, and that's sayin' something. Didn't you do a couple of jobs for him back when he was a Montana lawman?"

That brought up some old memories. Some I would like to forget. I looked away from his gaze remembering those times. I always got my man. Except for that last one.

Looking back at the marshal I said, "Yeah, I helped him out a few times, but that was long ago and far away. Different country. Tracking a man through muskeg swamps is a whole nuther story." Standing up to leave I added, "I reckon you'll have to find someone else."

As I started to turn toward the door, marshal Sullivan said, "NO!"

I turned my head and met his gaze. "What do you mean, 'no'?"

"Just that. No. I don't want anybody else. I want you."

I turned and faced him squarely. "Marshal, what you want, what you need, is a tracker who is competent." The words just flowed out of my mouth and I could not stop myself. "The last job I was on, the bad guy got away from

7

me. He ended up killing four more people. Good people. A farmer, his wife and two little kids. If I'd have done my job competently, they would still be alive."

Well, there it was, all out in the open.

Marshal Sullivan stared at me for a few seconds then said in an even tone, "None of us, and I mean none of us are perfect."

'Yeah, here comes the preaching,' I thought to myself. However, I sensed something in his words. Perhaps he, too, lived with a memory he would just as soon forget.

"What makes you think you're so special?" he continued. "We can all look back on our lives and regret something we did or didn't do. Now quit feeling sorry for yourself. Pick yourself up, dust off your britches and climb back in the saddle. Besides..." Sullivan paused as he picked up a piece of paper on his desk, "this copy of the Judge's order he signed last fall when you were after Jon Batiste says, and I quote, '...until such time as his services are no longer needed." Sullivan tossed the paper back on his desk. "Your services are needed."

He had me in a corner. I stared into his eyes for a few moments then realized he was not going to back down.

"Can I at least go home and say goodbye to my new bride?" I asked.

"Sorry, but no. The train leaves for Cha-tanika in an hour."

Sullivan shuffled through the papers on his desk, picked one up, and handed it to me.

"Here's your ticket to ride," he said.

CHAPTER 2

I STEPPED OUT OF THE SHERIFF'S office and started to cross the street. The only thing on my mind was Corrine and how she was going to take this. Suddenly, someone grabbed my arm and pulled me back just as a roaring, grunting, smoke belching horseless carriage bounced and slid down the muddy street I had been standing in. I looked back to thank the person who had just saved my life from that roaring beast. It was Freddie from Freddie's Barbershop.

"Thanks," I said. "And what the heck was that?"

Freddie laughed and said, "That's Bobby Sheldon in his Pope-Toledo touring car he just brought in from Dawson. He has plans on using it as a stage to Valdez and back."

"Really?"

"Yup."

I turned my head and watched it bounce down Cushman Street, rear tires spinning mud as people ran to get out of his way. I had seen one or two around town the last couple of years, but I never paid them any mind. They always looked way too dangerous to me.

I made my way to the telegraph office and sent Corrine at Salchaket a message about what was going on. She was in the middle of teaching school but was able to answer before I caught the four-o'clock train to Chatanika. She wished me good luck, and then she added, "Keep watch for *shoh*," which, in her mother's tongue means 'bear'. I thought that was sweet of her to be concerned, but I always kept a clean camp and never tempted fate in bear country.

Watching the Tiega slip by the coach window, veiled in wisps of coal smoke and cinders from the locomotive, I thought about what the marshal had said. I guess he was right. It was childish the way I had been behaving. I just could not get the fact out of my head that that farmer and his family were dead because of me. Because of something, I had missed. Some sign the killer had left behind.

"Get back on the horse," he had said, or something to that effect. It had been a long time since I had tracked a man. I thought to myself, '*Huh...easier said than done. Well, good or bad, I'm on the iron horse now, riding this thing to the end. One way or another, I have to catch this killer.'*

* * *

The train pulled into Chatanika at four forty-five p.m. on the dot, as the conductor announced that this was the end of the line. I made my way off the terminal platform and down the muddy street, dodging horse-drawn carriages and dog teams pulling carts.

The buildings were a hodge-podge of hastily built structures. Some made of logs, some frame built with either board and batten siding or clapboards.

Marshal Sullivan had called ahead to the miners' hall and asked them to call a miners meeting upon my arrival.

After checking into Smyser's Hotel, I made my way to the meeting hall. Claud Springer, the President of the Miners Association, met me at the door.

"You must be Dalton Laird," he said, looking me up and down.

He was a rotund person, about five-feet-six, I figured, wearing a brown suit jacket, corduroy pants, and a derby hat. His right index finger hooked a stogie he used to punch holes in the air as he talked.

"I am."

"Heard about your run-in with Jon Batiste

last fall. I'm glad somebody finally stood up to that character. Come on in."

He turned, stuffed the stogie in his mouth, then took off his hat and led me between rows of chairs to the front of the small meetinghouse.

"A lot of the boys are here already. Others are out working their claims. Gotta make hay while the sun shines, don't cha know. Don't know what else we can tell ya that ain't' already been said to the deputy," Claud said as he hung his hat and jacket on a hat tree in the corner of the room.

'*That's probably true, but we'll see*,' I thought.

I hung my hat next to his and we sat down at the table, facing the crowd.

Claud banged his gavel on the table, stood up and called the meeting to order then introduced me.

"Gentleman, this here is Dalton Laird. He came to hear what we might have to say about the goin's on, here of late. So, without further ado, I'll let him speak."

Claud sat down and looked at me.

I had not prepared any speeches and did not know quite where to start. However, I had to come up with something fast. I do not like crowds and I am not one for public speaking, so I decided on the next best thing.

Staying seated, I said, "I want to talk with whoever found the bodies in the river and the lone miner in his camp last fall. If need be, I'll contact a few others of you later."

Two men raised their hands.

"You, in the blue checked shirt," I said, pointing to one of the men.

"I found one of 'em. Floated right up on shore where I was sluicing."

"Okay," I said. "And what about you," pointing to the other miner.

"I found one caught in a sweeper about a mile upstream from my claim."

"Okay. Anyone else?"

"Old man Higgins found George in his camp last fall," someone said from the back of the room. "But he ain't here. He's out working his claim."

"Alright," I said as I pointed to the two who had raised their hands. "I want you two to stay. The rest of you gentlemen can leave."

As everyone got up to leave, I turned to Claud and said, "Get me the map of George's claim. I may want to take a look-see around his camp."

* * *

The interviews didn't last long, and by six fifteen, I wasn't any further than when

I had started. I was getting hungry and said as much to Claud as we stepped out onto the boardwalk.

He pointed to a little restaurant down the street and said I could find good grub there. "Of course," he continued, "it ain't Delmonico's, and it's the only one in town, but they have a decent cook."

I entered the front door, stepped to the side, and quickly gave the room a once-over. Two long tables, end-to-end, filled with hungry miners, took up the middle of the wallpapered room. Two electric chandeliers hung from the ceiling. As luck would have it, a couple of small empty tables sat in the back by the kitchen door with a good view of the room and the front door. That was more to my liking.

Several pairs of eyes followed me as I made my way to the table. I noticed, too, the patrons seemed pretty quiet. Quieter than usual for a room full of hungry men.

The waiter showed up in a white shirt, black vest, black bow tie, and slicked back hair, parted in the middle.

"What'll ya have?" he asked.

"I'll have the...," I began when suddenly someone shouted from across the room.

"Waiter, we need some more coffee."

We both looked in the direction of the

voice. A rough looking individual was standing at the long table looking at us.

"I'll be there in a minute," the waiter said. I looked the individual up and down. He started to say something but made eye contact with me, and evidently decided it was not that important. He sat back down.

"Jeez, I hate it when people interrupt me," I said half aloud as I looked up at the waiter. He looked back at me and grinned.

"You're Dalton Laird, aren't you?"

"Yeah."

"Thought so. I've heard of you."

I glanced back at the miners at the long table and said, "Well, don't believe everything you hear."

"Oh, it's all good."

I looked back into his eyes. "Like I said..."

I finished giving him my order, the impatient miner got his coffee, and fifteen minutes later, I got my food. By that time, some of the men had finished, paid their tab in gold dust and left. As I slowly ate my meal, the rest of the men finished and drifted on. By the time I finished eating, there was no one left but the busboy, the waiter, and me.

As I paid my bill and noted it in my ledger for the marshal, I casually asked the waiter if everyone pays in gold.

"Usually. Placer gold. Some pay with greenbacks."

Placer gold. That caught my attention. '*Why did he specifically mention placer gold? That's all there is around here.*' Maybe, someday, somebody will strike a rich vein and start hard rock mining. Right now, placer mining is the way to go.

"Why did you specifically mention placer gold?" I asked him.

"Well, I don't know..." he began as he looked down at the counter-top for a couple of seconds. Then, looking back at me he continued, "I guess it's because some guy paid a couple of times last fall, and then again earlier this spring, with what he said was hard rock gold when I asked him about it. It was rough and angular, somewhat wiry. I'm no miner, but I do know gold when I see it."

"Did it have bits of other rock attached to it?"

"No, sir. It looked really pure, so I accepted it."

I had a good idea what it was.

"You know who this person is?" I asked.

The waiter shook his head. "No, I don't. All I know is he always wore a black bear robe when he came in here. So I just started calling him 'Bear Robe Man'".

"Bear Robe Man, huh?"

"Yep."

"Anything else?"

The waiter looked down at the counter-top again, as if thinking about it, then said, "Well...I saw him with someone else a few times." Then, looking back at me, he continued, "A skinny, nervous fellow. Always seemed to be on edge."

"Got a name?"

The waiter pursed his lips together, glanced around the room, looked back at me, shrugged his shoulders, and said, "No. Sorry."

I believed him.

"Okay. Well, thank you for your time. If you think of anything else, let me know," I said as I handed him a tip. Then I turned and headed for the door.

CHAPTER 3

THE NEXT MORNING, I LOOKED up Mr. Springer, the Miners Association president. After picking up the map of the claim where the miner was found murdered, George Pickford his name was, I asked Claud if he knew of anyone who matched the description the waiter had given me. He said he recognized the description of the skinny one and produced a map of his claim as well. Henry Cravats was the name recorded. No mention of a partner. The claim was three miles upstream on the Chatanika, across from the mouth of Poker Creek. I decided it was a good day for a stroll, so I headed in his direction.

On the way out of town, I decided to stop by the telegraph office and send Yukon Jack a message to meet me here in Chatanika tonight. After I arrested Bear Robe Man and marched him back to town, I would not mind Jack's help in getting him back to Fairbanks for questioning.

The mosquitoes were a bit troublesome and I wished I had had the foresight to bring a head-net. However, I hadn't, so I just kept swishing them away from my face so I wouldn't inhale one, and kept moving.

I soon reached a clearing on the bank of the river. A small cabin was smack dab in the middle. The door faced the river and a small window stood just to the left of the door.

"HELLO THE CABIN!" I yelled as I made my way to the door.

I started to knock, but then I noticed the briefest movement through the window. A face appeared and then was gone. Expecting the door to open and be greeted, I stopped. And waited. Nothing.

"Hello the cabin," I yelled again. "I'm Dalton Laird looking for Henry Cravats. Can we talk?"

Again, nothing. I did not like this at all. Whoever was inside could see me perfectly well. I could not see them, so, I put my back against the log wall on the right side of the door, away from the window, and wondered what to do. I didn't have to wait long.

I heard the door latch unlock, followed by the slightest squeak of the door hinge. Slowly turning my head to the right, I watched with my peripheral vision as a shotgun barrel slowly eased out between the door and the jamb. I took a deep breath and with one fluid movement, reached up with my right hand, grabbed the shotgun barrel, and shoved it up toward the top of the door jamb. With it pinned against the jamb, I ducked, spun to the right, and slammed into the door with all my weight.

The shotgun went off, the door flew open, and I found myself inside the cabin holding the barrel of a single shot twelve-gauge shotgun.

My ears were ringing from the concussion of the muzzle blast. As my eyes adjusted to the dim interior, I saw a tall skinny man backed up against the far wall, holding his bloody nose.

"Well, that was a fine 'How-do-ya-do'. You always greet visitors that way?" I asked, as I stuck a finger in one of my ears and wiggled it around, trying to clear out some of the ringing.

He mumbled something unintelligible.

"What? I can't hear you." I said as I rested the shotgun against the wall.

Speaking louder he said, "I usually don't get many visitors."

"Well, no wonder. What's your name?"

"Henry." He said as he pinched his nose, trying to stop the bleeding.

By now, some of the ringing had subsided. "Henry, what?"

"Cravats. Henry Cravats."

Looking quickly around, I saw a rag lying

on the table. "Here," I said as I tossed it to him. "You're getting blood all over yourself."

Henry flinched as if I was going to hit him again.

"Aw, take it easy and have a seat."

"Just don't hit me again, mister," he whined.

"I ain't going to hurt ya. Not unless ya try to pull another fool stunt."

He sat down, wrapped the rag around his nose, and then pinched his nostrils shut. "You darn near broke my nose," he said.

"And you darn near blew my head off. Consider yourself lucky," I said as I sat down at the table facing him.

Henry pulled the rag away from his nose and checked the bleeding. It had stopped. As he wiped the blood off his hands he said, "Well, now that you're here, what do you want? If it's gold, you're out of luck. The pickin's is slim-to-none. What little I had saved up, the last 'visitor' stole."

I kind of felt sorry for this fella.

"No, it's not the gold I'm wanting, it's information. I've been told you have a partner who wears a bear robe all the time."

Henry gave a little snort. Some blood bubbled out of one nostril. He quickly wiped it off as his eyes darted around the room.

"He ain't no partner of mine. Not on paper anyways," he said as he quickly glanced out the door then back at me. "He thinks he is. Came in here one day and made himself at home. Talked about how his last partner double-crossed him. Then he made a few veiled threats that left no doubt in my mind what would happen if I objected. He always seems to have gold, though. Course, chunky stuff."

"What's his name and where can I find him?" I asked.

"Don't know his name; he never said, and I never asked. He's supposed to be up on Poker Creek, just across the river there, prospecting a new claim, and building a cabin."

"You expect him back soon?"

"A couple more days. He's probably running short of supplies."

"How far is it to the claim?"

"Four miles from the mouth."

'Well, another four-mile hike,' I thought. Quickly calculating, I figured I could get to the second cabin, take Bear Robe Man into custody, and march him back to Chatanika in time to meet Jack. All told, a fourteen-mile round trip. 'I might not have to do any tracking after all.'

Then I thought about Mr. Cravats.

"Maybe it's best you head into town. If I miss Bear Robe Man on the trail or something, and he comes back here, he's gonna know you talked. At least in town, you'll be safe."

"Oh, no. I don't feel safe out there in the open."

I shook my head, stood up, and said. "Suit yourself."

CHAPTER 4

THE FOUR-MILE HIKE UP POKER Creek went well, except for the stupid mosquitoes. I think I lost a half-pint of blood by the time I got to a cabin that fit Henry's description.

I stood in the willows downstream from the cabin and watched it for a while to find out the lay of things. Smoke rose from the stovepipe sticking out of a low sod roof. Someone was around. Soon, a big man came out of the outhouse in back and to the right of the cabin. He was wearing a black bear robe. In actuality, it was more like a Mexican serape, with a hole cut in the center of the pelt for the man's head to fit through. The head of the black bear and fore paws hung in front, and the tail and hind paws hung in back.

'*This has to be my man*,' I thought.

After taking a careful look around himself, he made his way to the cabin. Something about the way he walked bothered me. Just in front of the door, he stopped and once again looked around. Either he had a feeling someone was watching him, or he was being overly cautious.

I instinctively ducked behind a larger bush. Easing back around to get a better view, I saw him open the cabin door, walk in, and close it behind himself.

I needed to question this man about the murders, but as I stood there, I realized I should have brought some backup. My best chance alone would have been catching him in the outhouse, but that chance was gone. I decided I would just play the hand I was dealt and see where it goes. I wished I had my rifle.

I gave it about ten minutes, unsnapped and loosened up the Colt in its holster, took a dip of Copenhagen, then made my way to the clearing, and stood by a good-sized spruce tree. I 'helloed' the cabin, the door opened a crack and a deep voice answered back.

"Who are you and what do you want?"

"Name's Dalton Laird and I want to talk to you."

"What about?" The voice sounded like he was irritated.

"It's about some dead miners with missing teeth. Know anything about it?" I asked.

"I don't know nothin' and I ain't got nothin' else to say. Now get off my claim."

I tried reasoning with him. "It won't take

long. You might have seen or heard something that might answer some of my questions."

Raising his voice he said, "I told ya, I don't know nothin'. Now GET!"

I decided to push it a little, "I hear tell ya got some queer lookin' gold ya carry around. Hard rock gold ya call it."

Suddenly I caught the glint of light off a polished gun barrel as he thrust it through the open doorway into daylight. I pulled the Colt and ducked behind the spruce just as a bullet peeled bark and sprayed shrapnel past my chest.

'Well, so much for plan 'A'.'

"ALRIGHT, ALRIGHT. I'M LEAVIN'," I yelled. "NO NEED TO GET HOSTILE!"

I re-holstered the Colt, stuck both hands out from behind the tree so he could see they were empty, then backed into the brush, keeping the tree between us.

"I'M LEAVIN'," I yelled again.

Fifteen feet from the tree, I was concealed well enough that I knew he couldn't see me. I turned then and made it another hundred yards or so, then sat down by the creek and swished mosquitoes from my face. The shakes from the adrenaline rush started as I sat there chastising myself for not bringing back-up in the first place.

I washed my hands in the ice-cold creek

water, cupped them, and took a good long drink. Then I untied the bandanna from my neck, rinsed it in the cold water, and wiped my face and the back of my neck. That seemed to help settle me down some.

'*Obviously, Bear Robe Man does not want to talk,*' I thought to myself. Perhaps he had something to hide. I had a hunch what that something was.

I reached down and swished the bandanna in the cold creek water again, then rung it out and mopped my face one more time with one hand, while swishing mosquitoes from my head with the other.

I did not believe I would be able to get him out of the cabin by myself, and I wished I had just waited until Yukon Jack was here. The only weapon I was carrying was the revolver with twelve rounds of ammo, and no food. I was unprepared.

'*Well, nothing else to do but go back to Chatanika and pick up Yukon Jack,*' I decided. '*More than likely, this guy is going to run as soon as he realizes I'm really gone. Then it is going to turn into a tracking job for sure.*' I just wished I knew what it was that was so familiar about him.

CHAPTER 5

I WALKED INTO SMYSER'S HOTEL WHILE scratching the mosquito bites on my face and neck, and found Yukon Jack sitting in the parlor holding up a newspaper.

"Hello, big guy," he said as he briefly glanced over the top at me, and then back down at the paper.

"Been out traipsin' around the bush I see."

I looked down at myself. My pant legs were still damp from crossing the river and a couple of creeks, and my boots squished when I walked.

"Got et up by the skeeters, too, didn't ya?" he continued. "Why didn't ya bring a head net?"

I sighed, "Jack, don't even start."

He folded up the paper, tossed it aside, looked at me with his one good eye, and said, "Start? I ain't begun to start. We's supposed to be partners, Why didn't ya get ahold of me sooner?"

Jack seemed a little perturbed. I studied the scar and stitches that ran like a centipede track from the top of his left ear to the cheekbone, over his left eye, then disappeared into the hairline in the middle of his forehead. Ever since that day last fall when I saved his life after he was mauled by that grizzly, he always watched over me like a big brother. Even after Corrine and I got married, I had to shoo him away so we could have our honeymoon.

"Sorry Jack," I said. "There was no time to let you know. I barely had time to wire Corrine to let her know I wouldn't be home for supper, and then catch the train. Besides, I thought maybe I could have this wrapped up today or tomorrow by the latest. As it turns out, that's not gonna be the case. You got a room yet?"

"Yeah, it's next to your'n."

"Well, let's go upstairs to your room and I'll fill you in on what's happened so far," I suggested.

"Good, then I can show ya my surprise."

'Surprise? Now what has he done', I wondered. Before I had time to ask, Jack headed up the stairs.

Jack opened up his door and stepped inside. I followed, stepped to the left, and immediately caught movement from the corner of my eye of something big and furry coming at me fast. I tried to make a fist, cock back, and get ready for a roundhouse punch. I was too slow. Whatever it was, landed both paws on my shoulders, pinned me to the wall, and licked me from chin to forehead. Then I heard Yukon Jack cackling like a barnyard hen, and I realized he was laughing and trying to push the beast off me.

Between fits of laughter, I heard him say "Get down...that's no way to treat guests...lay down." Then, turning to me, he said, "What do ya think of my new dog?"

"Dog? He's as big as a horse. Well, maybe a Shetland," I said as I pulled out my bandana and wiped dog slobbers off my face.

Jack stopped laughing, but a big grin was on his face.

"Ain't he purty? A Malamute. Two years old!"

I could see he was proud of his...horse-dog, so I tried to be congenial, even though I wasn't really enthused about it.

"I, um, wasn't really expecting to have to provide for and take care of a...," I looked over at the malamute lying on the floor, panting puffs of warm doggy breath I could feel through my pant leg. Looking back at Jack I continued, "...a dog on this trip."

"Don't you worry none about him, young-un. He's my dog, I'll take care of him. Besides, he can provide for hiself. He's smart and a quick learner. And another thing, I got a dog pack for him in the deal. He can haul a thirty-pound load all day long."

'*Hmm...*' I thought to myself. '*That puts a new spin on things.*'

"Alright. Just keep...What's his name?"

"Kitty."

"Kitty?"

Jack shook his head matter-of-factly, and said, "Kitty."

I was confused, but intrigued, "Okay. I give. Why do you call him Kitty?"

"On account, he reminds me of Klondike Kate back in Dawson. Everybody called her Kitty. The way his fur moves when he runs, reminds me of her dancing at Pantages Orpheum with all those fur boas."

I was speechless. I did not know what to say. I kind of thought maybe he was going a little 'bushy' on me. Vestiges of cabin fever. Finally, I said, "Just keep *Kitty* off me, ya hear?"

Jack smiled and said, "I knew you'd see it my way."

CHAPTER 6

THE NEXT MORNING I WAS in a hurry to go. I was concerned Bear Robe Man might not stay at the cabin and decide to run. If he had run, I did not want him to get too much of a head start. I wanted him to feel my presence behind him, pressuring him into carelessness; making mistakes.

I pounded on Jack's door.

"SIX O'CLOCK. TIME TO GET UP," I hollered.

"It's too early, consarn it," he growled.

"The sun's been up for three hours, we're burnin' daylight."

After breakfast, I bought supplies at N. Jaffe's Clothier store, across the street from the hotel, and at R.M. Courtnay's General Merchandise. These, I noted in the ledger for the marshal, and equally distributed in the rucksacks for me, Jack, and Kitty the dog. I made sure to get head nets for Jack and me, and he bought a concoction of Hudson's Bay tea, mint and wormwood oil, said to keep mosquitoes at bay. We will see.

Jack had brought my new sporterized version of a 1903 Springfield and a box of 30.06 shells for me. He carried a 12 gauge with an assortment of buckshot and slugs. Both rifles *skookum* medicine against hungry spring bears just coming out of hibernation. The Colt I left with the hotel clerk in a safe, until my return. I did not want to carry the extra weight.

Two hours later, we crouched down at the edge of the clearing and observed Henry Cravats' cabin for signs of activity. It was quiet. There was no smoke from the chimney, and the door stood half-open. A sense of heaviness lay over the surroundings. A couple of chickadees flitted through the branches, but even they held their tongue.

I took off my pack and head net and motioned for Jack to do the same.

Talking in almost a whisper I said, "Stay inside the tree line and work your way to the right. I'll go to the left. When I give you the signal, we'll work our way to the side of the cabin. Stay away from the door and any windows."

When I got into position, I could see Jack on the other side of the clearing. The back of the cabin looked clear, so I gave him the signal.

A couple of minutes later, Jack and I were peaking at each other from opposite corners of the front of the cabin. I crouched low to work my way under the front window to the door. About now, I was wishing I had the revolver for close quarters work. '*Oh well, here goes nothing.*'

I stood up, put the rifle to my shoulder in the low ready position, took a step, then spun to my left, and kicked the door open. My rifle came up to the ready position and I quickly scanned the interior looking for movement.

Nothing. All was quiet and still, so I took a step inside.

As my eyes adjusted to the darker interior, I saw a pair of legs sticking out from under the overturned table next to the bunk at the back of the cabin.

I stepped aside to let Jack in, then turned my head and motioned to Jack with a nod to the table. Jack grabbed the table leg and pulled it back. I stood ready to fire if need be.

It was evident Henry Cravats was dead. He lay face down, stiff as a board.

"I warned him yesterday to leave and go back to town," I told Jack. "But he wouldn't listen."

"Well...now what?"

"Help me roll him over," I said as I knelt down and laid the rifle on the bunk.

When we got him on his back, it was evident he had taken a serious beating. His face was bruised and dried blood had oozed out of his ears, mouth, and nose. I could not find any evidence of a gunshot wound. I figure he probably died of a brain hemorrhage or internal bleeding. Suddenly I noticed his left hand, closed in a fist, held something black, like fur, sticking out between his fingers. I reached down and pulled some free. On closer examination, I realized what it was... black bear fur.

Jack and I searched the cabin and cache for evidence of next of kin for Henry. I found a letter from a woman in Ohio who, in the context of the letter, seemed to be related. Probably a sister. I confiscated the letter and stuffed it away for safekeeping.

I was anxious to get on the trail of Henry's killer. I did not want to spend another four hours backtracking to Chatanika to send a wire to the US Marshal to retrieve the body. The sooner I got on the killer's trail, the sooner I could bring him in.

I picked up my rifle and leaned it against the wall so we could put Henry on his bunk and cover him with blankets until our return. We closed the cabin up and I wrote a note stating, in effect that this was a crime scene, and that no one was to enter under penalty of law. I signed my name, and then nailed the note to the door.

I began searching in front of the cabin in half circles from the left side of the cabin to the right, trying to pick up tracks that were different from mine, Jack's, and Henry's. Soon, I found a couple of indistinct prints, headed toward the river and Poker Creek beyond. The left print turned inward, and I remembered Bear Robe Man had walked with a limp when I observed him walk from the outhouse to the cabin yesterday.

Looking around, I saw Jack was close to our packs.

"Jack, pack up and bring mine. I found him."

At the river near the bank, a muddy area showed clearly Bear Robe Man's tracks. I cut a willow wand and placed the tip on the back edge of the heel of the left footprint, then cut a notch in the willow at the front edge of the toe of the right footprint. Still holding it in place, I cut another notch further down the wand that touched the heel of the right footprint. The distance between the two notches indicated his shoe size. From the tip of the willow wand to the second notch represented his average stride. If I ever lost the next print, the wand would indicate where to focus my attention. Next, I made a quick sketch on graph paper of the boot track and the pattern of the soles for future reference. His left foot turned inward distinctly.

We donned our head nets because of the mosquitoes, crossed the Chatanika, and headed up the muskeg flat of Poker Creek toward the cabin. After about a mile, I became concerned about possible ambush.

"Jack, I want you to angle up the side of that ridge-line and make your way upstream until we get to the cabin. I'll stay on track. Stay about fifty yards ahead of me and always in sight. Keep an eye out and signal me if you see anything suspicious."

"Gotcha," he said.

I waited and watched as he and Kitty made their way through the brush and onto the side of the ridge. Once in place, I gave the signal to advance. I was not concerned about track to track tracking, because I knew Bear Robe Man was ahead of us, and I had a good idea he would be at the cabin..., or at least, that was my hope.

An hour and a half later, we reached the clearing. A fifteen-minute observation revealed no activity and I became concerned he had run.

"HELLO THE CABIN," I yelled. "THIS IS DALTON LAIRD, THE CABIN IS SUR-ROUNDED," I lied. "COME OUT WITH YOUR HANDS UP."

Nothing.

Yukon Jack and I went through the same

scenario as we had with Henry's cabin, except this door was closed and latched on the inside. As Jack and I peeked at each other from the opposite corners of the cabin, I could see the latch-string was out. Either he wanted us to open the door, or he was not here. Only one way to find out I guess.

With weapons at high ready, we pulled the latch-string, slammed the door open, and entered.

Bear Robe Man was gone.

CHAPTER 7

THE STOVE WAS COLD, BUT inside the firebox, buried deep in the ashes, one or two live embers glowed when uncovered. Obviously, it had been hours since the last fire burned.

"Well, it looks like he's got a pretty good head start," I told Jack. "But why would he run unless he knew for sure I would be back?"

Jack shrugged his shoulders.

"Guilty conscience? Maybe he didn't want to take any chances."

"Maybe," I said.

"Or...maybe he's heard of you. He may even know you," Jack mused.

That was an intriguing possibility. I had to admit that something had been puzzling me all day about the track itself, but I could not quite piece it together. Something about that turned in footprint created an anger that smoldered beneath the surface like the embers in that stove.

I pulled out my watch and looked at it. It read one-thirty.

"We still have about eight hours of daylight. Stay here at the cabin and fix us something to eat. I'll scout around and try to work out his direction of travel," I told Jack.

Bear Robe Man's tracks, of course, were all over the place. After a half hour of following dead ends and, curiously, finding bits of black bear fur stuck on limbs and brush wherever he walked, I got to thinking, "What would I do if I wanted to get away? I'd let nature help hide my tracks then head for the ridge-line where it's faster walking and I could watch my back trail."

I followed the creek upstream about fifty yards and found the bank caved in a little. Sure enough, I found a fresh print where he had climbed up out of the creek and into the thick brush. Why would someone do this unless he was trying to hide his tracks? Bits of bear hair proved his passage. A few yards later, an overturned stone and some broken twigs confirmed I was on track. Looking up and ahead, I could see a large birch growing amongst some spruce near the ridge-line. Woods wonderers have a tendency to pick out landmarks and work toward them. I was convinced Bear Robe Man was heading toward that birch and the ridge-line.

I marked the spot by tying my bandanna

to a tree limb, and then made my way back to the cabin. Jack was just finishing up with the meal. He had caught some nice grayling, a couple of which were now frying in the skillet, and to accompany that, fresh sourdough biscuits and rice. I was starved. I removed my head net so I could eat and began swishing mosquitoes away from my face. Jack tossed me the concoction he had bought.

"Try this. It works pretty good."

I rubbed some on my face and the back of my bit-up neck then started to eat.

"I found his tracks," I said to jack with a mouth full of half-chewed food. "I think I know where he's headed."

Jack looked at me with a slight grin, picked up his tin cup of water, and said, "Where's that?"

Jack took a drink of water as I swallowed my food. Then I explained, "I figure he's headed for the ridge-line. Tracks are leading in that direction. It's easier walking."

Jack put his cup down.

"Makes sense to me. What's me and Kitty's part in this, besides being a pack mule?"

"Well, I'm going to have you doing a very important job. You're going to be protecting me from ambush. Most of my attention will be focused on locating sign and working out his trail. Just like we did coming up here to the cabin, I'm going to need you ahead and to my right. Concentrate on spotting Bear Robe Man up ahead. If I start working toward you, stop.

"You may have just crossed his tracks. If I start working away from you, you'll have to scramble to get back in line with me. Other than that, you can be the camp cook as well. Now let's stuff the rest of this food down our gullet and get packed up. The more we dilly-dally, the more distance he gains."

With lunch over, we packed up and headed for the spot I had marked with my bandana.

I pointed out the birch tree I guessed Bear Robe Man headed to and started working out the tracks as Jack worked his way into position.

Fifteen minutes later, I couldn't find another track. I began to panic. The last time this happened, things did not turn out well.

'*You've lost your touch*,' I told myself. '*No, think. Something is there; you just have to find it.*'

Working my way backward, I examined the tracks that I had found coming up out of the creek. Looking at them closely, I realized they did not look right. The toe dig, the divot created when a person pushed off for the next step, was missing. The tracks were too flat. Then I realized Bear Robe Man had walked backward in his own tracks. He had taken four or five steps up on the bank, and then carefully stepped in his own tracks back into the creek.

"So...," I said aloud as if I were talking to him, "obviously you're a crafty fellow. You have some knowledge of anti-tracking techniques."

Scanning the other bank, I looked for sign he may have gone that way instead. Nothing. That left the creek bottom, in the water, as the only route he could have taken.

I worked my way northward, upstream, and soon found a smear of mud on the top of a large rock sticking out of the waters flow. Later, I found a small oblong rock sticking up at a forty-five-degree angle out of the water. The top half was lighter colored than the bottom half. With all the water that had come down this creek during breakup, that rock should have been lying flat on the bottom, under water. Looking the rock over, I found the opposite end was pushed into a divot in the creek bottom sand. Something heavy had stepped on one end, shoving it into the soft sand, which lifted the other end up out of the water. A smile crossed my face. I was on track.

A smudge of mud here and a bear hair there with a broken willow limb now and then led us about two miles upstream. Then I found where Bear Robe Man's tracks left the stream again, this time to the left. Extra attention revealed these tracks were the real deal. Now the tracks were headed back southwest as he climbed a low hill at a forty-five-degree angle, working his way to the ridge-line.

Near the top, under a spruce tree, I found where Bear Robe Man had spent some time. Looking back the way I had just come, I realized what he had done. He had doubled back to watch his back trail. From this spot, he had a perfect view of the valley below that Jack and I had just worked our way up. Bear Robe Man now knows for sure that I am on his trail.

From the spot where I now stood, to the creek where Bear Robe Man would have first spotted me, I calculated to be about three hours of travel time. No telling how long he sat there watching us, but I decided to err on the liberal side and give him the full three hours head start. With this terrain and his estimated physical condition, I figure that put him about six to eight miles ahead of us.

I should have known better. I should have kept one eye on the horizon. Maybe I would have spotted his movement on the ridge-line. If I had, I could have cut some time and distance from his lead by abandoning his track for his last known position. I chastised myself and vowed to be more aware of my surroundings.

I heard a noise in the brush to my right. I turned and saw Yukon Jack and Kitty climbing the last few feet of the ridge to where I now stood. Jack was breathing kind of heavy.

He had picked up a diamond willow walking stick somewhere along the way, which he now used to lean on as he bent forward, coughed twice, and spat.

Between big lungfuls of air, he looked back up at me and said, "These ribs ain't used to this heavy breathin'."

I began to feel sorry for the old Sourdough, and I looked away and gritted my teeth as a whirlwind of thoughts blew through my brain. I should not have brought him along I guess, and I briefly contemplated sending him back to Chatanika. He was still mending from that grizzly attack last fall. '*But, darn it all, I need his help.*' Besides, I had gotten used to having him around. I rather liked his company. I just hoped he would not slow me down. I needed to close the distance on Bear Robe Man.

CHAPTER 9

"PARDNER," I SAID, "I SHOULDN'T have called you out here. I wasn't thinking, I guess. You still need more time to heal up."

I looked back at Jack. His eyes narrowed as he stared a hole through me, and I thought, '*Oh Lord, here it comes.*'

"Young-un, if you hadn't of called me, as soon as you got back, I would've kicked your butt. You know that don't cha?"

I tried to suppress a smile but could not.

"You would have tried."

Jack looked away, coughed again then spat.

"Well..., at least I would have given ya a good cuff upside the head," he said as he looked back at me. Then he smiled.

"Yeah, you probably would have," I conceded.

"Don't worry about me, young-un. I can

carry my own weight. I might be a little slow right now, but I'm good for the distance."

Of that, I had no doubt. I knew he would fight through this until the end.

"Now," he continued, "let's just stop this chit-chat and find this feller that's got you all tied up in knots inside."

"Is it that obvious?" I asked.

"Um-hum."

I thought a bit then decided on a plan.

"Jack, you and Kitty stay here. I'm going to scout around and pick up his trail. I've been thinking on it all afternoon, and I've a hunch he's going to stay away from the Circle City mail trail. Too many people. Nevertheless, he needs to get out of the country. Therefore, I think he's going to follow the ridges to Eagle Summit then drop down into Circle City on the Yukon and catch a stern-wheeler east to Dawson. I'm going to follow his tracks as fast and far as I can till sundown, about ten o'clock or so. I'll mark the trail plain for ya. When you catch your wind, follow along."

Jack pushed himself upright, but still leaned on the willow staff. He sounded like he was breathing easier already.

"What about being your protector?" he asked.

I sighed and looked around as my brain

sifted through all the information it had gained so far.

"That is a concern," I decided, "but, I think he just wants to travel. He feels confident in his abilities to get away." Looking back at Jack I added, "Somehow, and for some reason, I think this may even be a game to him."

It did not take long to pick up Bear Robe Man's trail further up the ridge. I stripped the limbs from the lower half of a young spruce sapling, and then bent the top half over until it snapped, then, let it lay in the direction of travel. Jack should be able to see that easily.

When traveling, people, like animals, tend to take the easiest route. Looking ahead, along the ridge top, I picked the most likely route and jogged about a hundred yards. Here, I stopped and looked for any disturbance. I soon spotted a dead, dry branch that had been broken in two, as if something had stepped on it. Using my stick, I measured the stride distance and looked for more sign. I soon spotted a green plant stem that had been crushed and flattened to the ground. I smiled. I was still on track.

The jogging and checking for sign went on most of the evening. The direction of travel had changed; I was now heading east. So far, my hunch had proven correct.

* * *

Along about eight o'clock, I found where Bear Robe Man had taken a side trip from a saddle between two hilltops, down to a spring. The ridge-line we were following swung a little south of east from this point on, creating sort of a bowl from which the spring bubbled up.

He had spent some time there resting. Of course, strands of bear hair stuck on some of the brush proved it was him.

All of the signs I read today indicated Bear Robe Man had walked this far. I, on the other hand, had jogged most of the way. I was sure I had gained a couple of miles on him. That would put me only four or six miles behind him.

I knew Bear Robe Man was tired. Who would not be after a full day of hiking?

Henry Cravats had mentioned that he thought Bear Robe Man was running low on supplies. Henry's cabin and cache had looked sparse, food wise.

I was betting Bear Robe Man was not packing much food, if any, forcing him to live off the land as much as possible. It was too early in the season for the wild berries. That meant eating snowshoe hare and spruce grouse, both of which were abundant.

A diet high in protein, low in fat with no carbohydrates. That could work to my advantage though, for a man could die of starvation with a belly full of rabbit.

There was only about an hour of daylight left, so before it got too dark, I scouted around the spring for sign of the direction Bear Robe Man had taken when he left. Thick sphagnum moss, Labrador Tea, blueberry bushes, stunted willow, and black spruce carpeted the ground. Unfortunately, I couldn't find a track or the inevitable stray bear hair.

Discouraged, I made my way back to the spring, filled my canteen, and then backtracked up into the larger, white spruce through which I had walked earlier. From there, while sitting under the spruce canopy, I could watch the spring and the ridge just beyond while I waited for Jack.

* * *

Forty-five minutes later, I heard someone to my left on my back trail, making his way to the saddle and the spring of water. I surmised it was Jack and gave a 'bob-white' whistle to get his attention. Evidently, it worked, because suddenly he was quiet. Another 'bob-white' whistle and he started moving in my direction.

Ten minutes later, Kitty ambled out of the darkening brush and gave me a slobbery lick upside the face. I was trying to quietly shove her away and make her behave when Jack walked up, dropped his pack, took Kitty's pack off her, and then plopped down beside me. He was breathing a little heavy, but no more than a man would after a day's hike toting a fifty-pound pack.

"Doin' alright?" I asked as I looked him up and down.

He stretched his legs out, leaned back against the tree.

"Oh, Yeah. Doin' fine. The gentle up-and-down slopes of the ridges ain't bad. It's the steep climb up here that gets to me."

I looked away out into the gathering gloom and followed the ridge-line with my eyes.

"If he stays on these ridges, I'll be able to gain on him I think. I figure I've already closed the distance by a couple of miles." Then, pointing off down the hill I added, "Tracked him to a spring in that bowl down there, but I lost the tracks. And, since it was close to getting dark, I decided to hole up till daylight. That'll give us about five hours of sleep."

"Sounds good to me," I heard him say through a yawn.

Looking back at Jack I asked, "How's your water?"

Jack reached over to his pack, grabbed the canteen, gave it a shake, and said, "There's a couple of slugs left."

"I've got a full canteen," I said. "It should last us through the night."

I was about to suggest we get something to eat when Jack said, "I been thinkin' about this here feller all day, you know, about the teeth and all? Well, it reminds me of Kantishna Carl. I ever tell ya about him?"

I smiled, as I scanned the fifty yards or so around us that was visible in the twilight, shook my head and said, "No, but I have a feeling I'm 'bout to hear it."

I looked back at him, and as he was digging through his pack for something to eat, he said, "The winter of 1900, I believe it was, he got scurvy real bad. Lost most of his teeth. But he pulled through, and when break-up rolled around, he was mighty tired of eatin' mush and soups and such. He got a hankerin' for meat. It just so happened that a young grizz, fresh out of hibernation wondered into his dog yard. Ol' Carl grabs his gun and the next thing ya know, that grizz is hanging on the meat pole.

"Well, now Carl has a problem. He's got a lot of steaks hangin' there, but no way to chew 'em. So he gets to thinkin' on it and decides to make a set of choppers. He spies an old Dall Sheep skull sittin' on his cabin roof and realizes the front teeth looks a whole lot like his used to. Well, that's a start, he figures, but what's he gonna use to hold 'em in place? Lookin' around, he finds an old soft tin cooking pot and decides to cut it up and use that for the bridgework. But he still has a problem. The sheep skull didn't have any molars. Aw, but the bear did. He dug those molars out, fitted 'em all together in the tin bridgework, and ate that bear with its own teeth."

I laughed in spite of myself. "Are you serious?"

"Serious as a heart attack," Jack said with a solemn look on his face as he handed me some smoked salmon.

My laugh had died down by then to a smile. I took the salmon and said, "Good ol' Yankee ingenuity."

Again, I scanned our surroundings.

"Somethin' botherin' ya?" Jack asked.

I looked back at him. "I don't know. Something just doesn't feel right."

Jack, Kitty, and I contented ourselves on the salmon, leftover sourdough biscuits, dried fruit and cold spring water for supper. I would have preferred hot tea, but I did not want to build a fire and risk giving our position away to Bear Robe Man. Not that I did not think he knew we were behind him, because he did. I just did not want him to know exactly where we were. Sort of hedging my bets, as it were.

I had thought most of the day about this person, this killer who wears a bear robe, trying to get inside his head. What makes a person do the things he is accused of? Why would a person kill people for a quarter ounce or less of gold filling in their teeth? I said as much to Jack.

Jack took a moment while he chewed on a piece of salmon. Then he swallowed and said, "I believe we're all born with a conscience. And if we have good parents, that conscience is nurtured and we learn right from wrong. We learn to have empathy for others. The Bible tells us we are all born with a will. We can exercise our will and choose to do right or wrong. If we choose to do wrong, our conscience convicts us. But, if we continue to choose to do wrong, our conscience becomes seared, like the Bible says, with a hot iron. It is no longer sensitive to the empathy of others.

"Bear Robe Man doesn't have a conscience. He's not normal. And that, young-un," Jack paused as he looked me in the eye, "makes him dangerous."

CHAPTER 10

I LET JACK SLEEP AS I took the first watch. Two and a half hours alone with my thoughts allowed my mind to drift.

I had told the Marshal that it had been years since I had tracked a killer and that I had not done a very good job of it. I had lost his trail. The sign was there, somewhere... but for the life of me, I could not find it, and he got away. I told him how, three days later, he ended up killing a farmer, his wife, and kids. That lady, her husband, and children paid for my mistakes. The proof was written in the bloody, turned-in left boot prints left behind. Much like...much like the prints I now followed.

I was stunned. Could it be? Could I be tracking the same man three thousand miles and ten years later? Again, a smoldering anger began to burn inside.

Suddenly, out of the corner of my eye, I thought I detected movement in the shadows of the night. But strain as I might, I could neither see nor hear anything out of place. Was it the past coming back? Or maybe my subconscious mind playing games? Or maybe a guilty conscience because I felt responsible for the death of that woman. And her husband. And the little girl. And the boy. I shuddered then, but I do not know why. Was it the chill night air?

Right then, I made a vow. I would not let this man get away. Whether he was the same person who killed them or not, I would not let him slip from my grasp to kill another.

Judging by the darkness, I guessed my time was up. I woke Jack, pulled my wool blanket out of my pack and bedded down on the spruce boughs Jack had piled up for his bed. But sleep eluded me as a thousand thoughts flitted through my brain.

During a quick breakfast, Jack asked, "What's on your mind, young-un?"

I told him of my thoughts the night before.

"So that's it," he said, as he nodded his head up and down.

"That's what?"

Jack looked at me and said, "That's what's been eatin' ya. I knew this feller was getting to ya somehow. Does he know who ya are?"

I looked out into the gathering light of day and once more scanned our surrounding.

"Yes," I said. "I announced who I was with my first encounter with him at the Poker Creek cabin."

"Are you even sure this is the same person? There's other people in the world that's pigeon-toed ya know. And if it is him, does he know you were the one tracking him all those years ago?"

I glanced back at Jack and shrugged.

"You're lettin' the past haunt you," he continued. "Last year you were holding a grudge against all of womankind, and you almost lost Corrine, the best thing that's happened to you. Now, you're holdin' a grudge against yourself. Young-un, ya gotta let it go. What's past is past."

"Jack, I can't let it go. I've got to prove to myself, if nobody else, I've still got what it takes to bring him or anyone else to justice. Call it pride, if you like, but I don't think I could live with myself if this one got away from me and killed someone else like the last one did. Two in a row? No. I ain't gonna let it happen."

We broke camp, headed down to the spring, and refilled our canteens. I left Jack there and backtracked up to the saddle, looking for any evidence Bear Robe Man had continued along the ridge-line.

Nothing.

Back at the spring, I told Jack to climb the saddle, and then follow the ridge that ran to the east and south and to keep an eye out for sign. If he found anything, he was to signal me and I would climb up to check it out. In the meantime, I would busy myself trying to work out where and how he left the spring.

After Jack left, I began to circle the spring, enlarging the circles with each pass, trying to find anything to indicate Bear Robe Man's passage. About an hour later and about fifty yards below the spring, in the rivulet of water, I found fresh mud smeared on some of the tundra and brush. Bear Robe Man had stepped in the mud then transferred it onto the plants as he walked along. That made me smile.

I looked up to the ridge-line to find Jack and let him know by sign that I was back on track. Instead, I saw Jack waving his arms, evidently trying to get my attention. Obviously, he had found something he thought was important.

Should I leave the obvious sign that Bear Robe Man was headed down the draw towards the Chatanika River and lose valuable time? Jack seemed insistent.

I took my bandana and ripped a strip of cloth off, then tied it to some tall brush nearby. This would help me locate the last known track if I had to come back. Then I climbed the hill up to Jack on the ridge-line.

"Gall darn it! Took ya long enough to check on me," Jack said as I huffed the last few steps to the top.

"Sorry," I said. "I was concentratin' on finding sign. Whatcha got?"

"Only his camp last night, is all. It's down the slope on the other side a few feet; just far enough to hide the light of his campfire from us on this side. But..." (Jack crooked his finger at me, beckoning me to follow as he walked away,) "...the son-of-a-gun sat right here behind this log, and watched us in our camp last night."

CHAPTER 11

FINDING BEAR ROBE MAN'S CAMP was a stroke of luck. The tracks he had laid downstream from the spring had me convinced he headed down to the Chatanika River and the mail trail to Circle City. Instead, he had traveled down the rivulet a ways, and then cut back sharply at a forty-five-degree angle back up to the ridge-line, ending up directly across the bowl with the spring to watch for us. There, he had made his camp.

Because Jack had taken the ridge-line around and found his camp, it had saved us four or more hours of work unraveling that little detail.

I made a quick scan of the area and something at the edge of the campsite caught my eye. I walked over to it.

"My hunch was right," I told Jack as I held up a fresh rabbit pelt lying next to its gut pile. "He's eating rabbit."

I looked at Jack. He shook his head and said, "Obviously he didn't shoot it, or we would've heard it. Must've snared it."

"Probably," I said as I dropped the pelt.

The gut pile aroused Kitty's interest and I let her lay claim to it as I walked back to the fire pit.

Squatting down, I cradled my rifle in my left arm and held my right hand over the ashes. It was still putting off a good heat.

"See any evidence of anything else he might have eaten?" I asked Jack as I looked around the fire pit.

"No, I didn't notice anything. Why?"

Just then, a couple of tufts of bear hair and rawhide strips lying next to the fire pit caught my attention. I decided to answer Jack's question first.

"Well, if I'm right, he's living off the land." I nodded my head over my shoulder to what was left of the gut pile. "Rabbit," I continued. Then I picked up the tufts of bear hair and rawhide, stood, and looked at Jack.

"That means he's going to have to take time out to hunt if he wants to eat. The easiest thing to get is rabbits. All protein. That kind of diet will fatigue him and he's going to start having trouble concentrating. Then he's going to get mighty thirsty and start looking for more water. However, he knows we're hot on his trail so that won't leave him much time to do that. He's also going to get more desperate. I think by now, he knows he's not going to shake us very easily. From here on out, he may try to ambush us, to give himself some relief."

"Young-un, he could've done that last night. He had the perfect opportunity behind that log. Why didn't he take it?" Jack asked as he sat down by the fire pit.

I looked down at him and said, "I don't know. I was kind of wondering that myself. Maybe he was just curious about us." I looked back down at the bear hair in my hand. "He's definitely playing games with us. I think he's got more tricks up his sleeve."

"Like what?"

Looking back at Jack, I said, "Some of the southwest Indians were known to wrap hides over their pony's hooves to broaden out their weight distribution. That tended to leave less of an imprint." I held up the tuffs of bear hair and rawhide strips. "I have a hunch Bear Robe Man just got the same idea. I think he cut up some of his bear robe to cover his boot soles. Of course, I won't know for sure till I look things over, but if he did, it's going to make tracking a lot tougher."

I tossed the bits of bear hair and rawhide strips onto the gray ashes of the fire pit and watched them curl and singe from the heat as I dug into my pants pocket for my Copenhagen.

Looking back at Jack I said, "I need you and Kitty to stay here while I scout around for sign. I don't want to take the chance of you two destroying any tracks he may have left. When I get things worked out, I'll let ya know." With that, I took a dip and replaced the Copenhagen in my pocket.

Figuring Bear Robe Man may have continued south down the ridge toward the Chatanika where there would be plenty of water, I started my search there. Search as I might, I found nothing to indicate his passage. Not even a stray bear hair stuck on a branch; my reliable 'tell' that confirmed all other sign.

I concentrated my search up the ridge, and, about a half mile north, then east, a brown colored rock caught my attention. It seemed out of place. Looking it over, I realized the brown color was caused by dampness. Turning it over revealed a dry, gray color. Next to the rock was a slight impression that fit perfectly the contour of the damp side of the rock. Closer examination revealed strands of bear hair. That made me smile.

Marking the spot with another piece of my bandana, I returned to Yukon Jack and Kitty and explained to him what I had found. As we hiked back to the rock, I mentioned again the need for water for Bear Robe Man and ourselves.

"Well, if I remember right..." Jack hesitated as if deep in thought. "There's a creek runnin' through a narrow canyon a few miles due east. I think this ridge drops down into it."

"You familiar with that country?" I asked.

"Did some prospecting in there a few years ago. It's a good place to hole up for a few days."

"How's that?"

"It's rocky and craggy. Lots of little side gullies a man could hide out in. Good fish in the creek too."

"I wonder if he knows about it?"

Jack stopped as I took a couple more steps, and then I stopped and looked back at him. He leaned on his diamond willow staff and said, "Do'no. But if I was him, that's where I'd go."

I took out my pocket watch and looked at it. Ten minutes until nine, it read.

I thought a bit and then said, "We've spent a little over four hours working this out. He's probably a good nine or ten miles ahead of us by now.

"If you're right about this ridge dropping down into that canyon, and if he's headed there, I could jog on ahead like yesterday and cut some more distance off his lead. It might be a risk but I think it's worth it. He thinks he's lost us with that trick he pulled. He won't be expecting us, and I might be able to locate him before he knows I'm there."

"Sounds like a plan."

"I'll make the trail plain for ya like I did yesterday," I said.

"If ya find him afore I get there, just don't do anything stupid. Wait for me. We'll take him together. Remember you got a pregnant young bride waitin' at home for ya."

"I won't do anything...wait...what?"

CHAPTER 12

LONG ABOUT NOON, I CAME upon some small outcropping of granite tors sticking up from the ridge. Tree line this far north is about three thousand feet, and I had left the tree line about an hour ago. At the base of the outcropping, I found some shelter from the occasional wind.

I rested my rifle against the rock, took my pack off, set it down, and then plopped down beside it. Taking my canteen out of the pack, I shook it to guesstimate how much was left. '*About half empty,*' I figured. '*Bear Robe Man probably has less.*' I took a swig and enjoyed the coolness of it in my mouth before swallowing. The breeze felt a little chilly, but at least there were no mosquitoes to contend with.

I looked along the ridge top as far as I could see before it disappeared behind a little knoll with another outcropping of granite. Something dark that seemed out of place caught my eye about a quarter of a mile away. I dug my binoculars out of the pack and gave it a gander. I could not make out much detail, so I made a mental note to check it out when I got there.

Lowering the binoculars, I laid them on top of my pack, leaned my head back against the rock, and closed my eyes.

Once again, the thought crossed my mind like it had a thousand times before during the past hours, '*I'm going to be a daddy*'.

Corrine's face flashed through my mind then. She was smiling at me, holding our baby. In turn, that made me smile. And my heart ached to be with her.

Jack had apologized. He said he was not supposed to say anything. It just sort of slipped out before he could stop himself. She had found out for sure the same day after I had sent her the telegram that I had a job to do.

I wanted off this ridge. I wanted to head south down Ptarmigan Creek to the Circle City mail trail, and then back west down the Chatanika to Fairbanks. However, I had a job to do and the sooner I got it done, the sooner I could be with my bride, the only family I had left.

I felt rested now, though my joints had stiffened up some. No matter. After a hundred yards of walking, they would limber up.

I found the dark colored object I had seen earlier through the binoculars. It turned out to be one of the pieces of bear hide Bear Robe Man had tied over one of his boots. It proved I was still on track. Evidently, it had come untied or worn off. Either way, Bear Robe Man did not bother retrieving it. He probably figured he was far enough away from me not to worry about it. I found the other one on the other side of the knoll that had blocked my view. Now tracking was a little easier.

I had a new spring in my step, and five hours later, I found myself looking down into a fairly steep and deep gorge running north and south. I felt confident that I had closed the distance on Bear Robe Man, so I set my pack down, dug out the binoculars, and studied every inch of the gorge looking for him.

From where I now sat, his tracks angled left, or toward the upstream portion. Downstream, a placer mining operation was in full swing. Evidently, Bear Robe Man did not want to take the chance of being seen by anyone and chose to avoid them.

Finally, about an hour later, I spotted movement along the opposite side of the creek, about a half mile upstream from my position. Closer observation revealed a man in a tattered bear robe working his way among the boulders strewn along the rushing creek. As I watched, at one point he stopped, looked around, and then seemingly disappeared into the canyon wall. Several minutes more of observation revealed no more movement.

I took out my notepad and pencil and quickly sketched the area, noting landmarks we could use later. About two hundred feet above where Bear Robe Man had disappeared, a bench of flat land ran east about a hundred yards to the foot of the next ridge-line.

I heard brush breaking behind me. Turning, I saw Yukon Jack and Kitty making their way down the ridge toward me.

Jack dropped his pack and sat down beside me. He and Kitty both were panting heavily.

"This the gorge you were telling me about?" I asked.

"Yep"

"There's a pretty good placer operation going on downstream," I said as I pointed in that direction.

Jack strained his neck as he looked around and through the brush to get a better look.

"Well, I'll be. The sons-o-guns must of found the paystreak I couldn't find. Well, that's life I guess." Jack turned back to face me. "What about Bear Robe Man? Any sign of him?"

I pointed off upstream. "Watched him disappear into the side of the canyon up there." Then I handed Jack my notepad.

"Made a sketch of the area from this vantage point."

Jack took it, looked it over, and then said, "There's a few clefts in the rock face. Can't see 'em from this angle. You have to almost walk up on 'em before ya see 'em. All of 'em as far as I know, go back a-ways, then dead ends. There's only one way out, and that's at the opening. If he's hidin' in one, we got 'im trapped."

I dug in my pocket for my watch, took it out and looked at it, then shoved it back into my pocket.

"It's four-fifteen p.m. What say we work our way down there, opposite of where I watched him disappear into the canyon wall? That will put us at about five o'clock, giving us about five hours before sunset. That should give us time to apprehend him and start marching him downstream to the placer mine. We could spend the night there, get a good meal, and then head out in the morning on the mail trail back to Chatanika."

Jack looked down at the ground for a minute, apparently in thought, then looked up at me and said, "With all that brush down there, it'll be pretty rough going. It's going to take you longer than you think to get to the bottom. Besides, me and Kitty need a rest. You've been here a spell. We just got here. Give us a half hour."

"How long you figure it'll take us to get down there?" I asked.

Jack looked down into the canyon. His eyes squinted a little. "An hour, at least"

Jack knew this part of the country, having prospected it before, so I gave him the benefit of the doubt. And, he was right of course. I had not thought about their needs.

'*So, an hour and a half and maybe more of daylight just to get to the bottom of the gorge. Then, we will need time to locate Bear Robe Man and formulate a plan based on whatever situation we find him and ourselves in. I want this thing to end and get back to Corrine as soon as possible*,' but it seemed just now the whole world was against me.

At about 6:00 P.M., we reached the bottom of the canyon. That left about four hours of daylight left. In addition, we still needed to locate Bear Robe Man, formulate a plan, take him into custody, and march him downstream to the placer mining camp. Preferably before sunset. If everything worked out right, we could do it. However, if anything went wrong, we could find ourselves stumbling downstream with a shackled prisoner in the dark. My mind said 'hold off till daylight', but my heart said 'get it over with and get back to Corrine.'

Bear Robe Man's tracks were plain in the muddy and sandy soil along the creek, and it was not long before I found where he had crossed the creek. About twenty-five yards upstream, I could see a cleft in the rock wall, across the creek, on the east side of the canyon.

Taking my binoculars out of my pack, I focused on the soft sandy soil in front of the entrance. A set of prints led into the cleft, then back out again to the creek, then back into the cleft.

"He's still in there," I whispered to Jack. "We've got him cornered."

"Well, what's it gonna be young-un? We just gonna go traipsin' into the opening of the cleft and ask him to come along peaceable like?" Jack asked.

I looked at Jack. He seemed to be getting a little surly.

"Well, no," I said. "I'm figurin' those walls are pretty much straight up and down in there. Not much in the way of cover. He starts shootin' at us, we won't have much to hide behind. I figure we'll set up on this side of the creek and watch the entrance. When he comes out to get water, wood, or whatever, then we'll make our move. One of us will cover him while the other puts the cuffs on him. See anything wrong with that?"

"What if he doesn't come out?"

"He's got to, sometime. If not this evening, then when it gets dark, or in the morning."

"Well, I'm not going to set here waitin' on that scum-bag to make the first move. My bellybutton's been shakin' hands with my backbone for a while now. I'll move back against the canyon wall about twenty yards, set up camp and fix us some grub. After I've eaten, I'll relieve ya so's you can eat," Jack said. Then he turned to leave without waiting for my answer.

'*Wonder what put a bee in his bonnet?*' I asked myself. I figured he was probably just hungry. Maybe those old grizzly wounds were bothering him. '*Oh well, no matter. He'll get over it,*' I decided.

I pulled out my pocket watch and looked at it. 6:37 P.M. I replaced the watch and turned my attention back to the cleft opening in the rock wall, just across the creek from where I sat concealed behind a couple of large boulders and brush, and waited. I was reminded of the old Peace Officers Axiom, 'Hours, and hours of boredom, interrupted by moments of sheer terror and panic.' I hoped it would not come to that.

About an hour and a half later, Jack returned.

"There's coffee and fresh sourdough bread wrapped around a stick baking by the fire. There's dried peaches and squaw candy too. Better go get ya some. I'll watch for a while."

I found the camp Jack had made and sat

down by the fire. After giving thanks for the Lord's providence, I ate with gusto. I must have been hungrier than I thought.

Just as I finished my second cup of coffee, I heard Yukon Jack yell "HANDS UP!," then the report of his double-barreled shotgun.

The blast echoed and reverberated from the narrow walls of the canyon and triggered an adrenaline rush that propelled me from my seat to my rifle.

The sharper *CRACK* of a bolt-action rifle and the angry whine of a ricocheting bullet overhead caused me to duck my head.

I shoved my rifle's safety off as I quickly picked my way through the brush and boulders toward Jack.

Another shotgun blast was followed quickly by the sharper report of a rifle.

I heard the bullet tear through the leaves and branches of the brush to my right, and I involuntarily ducked again.

I stumbled, regained my footing, and dove down beside Jack. He was reloading his shotgun.

Snapping the action closed, he looked at me and grinned.

"Almost had 'im!"

CHAPTER 13

"**W**HAT HAPPENED?" I ASKED JACK as I rolled to my right to look around the boulder to locate Bear Robe Man.

"Son-of-gun surprised me!"

I saw movement across the creek and threw a quick shot, left-handed, in Bear Robe Man's direction. Then I rolled to my left, onto my back. Out of the corner of my eye, I saw Jack spin to his left and rise up a little.

"How'd he surprise ya?" I asked as I worked the bolt action.

BOOM...BOOM Jack's shotgun barked.

I looked over at him as he plopped down beside me.

"Oh, I was just havin' a conversation with Kitty about how she's a good dog when I realize Bear Robe Man is standing on the other side of the creek with a canteen and a rifle..."

CRACK!

Bear Robe Man's rifle blast reverberated off the walls as the bullet, just inches above our heads, ricocheted off the top of the boulder, and sped off toward the rim rocks with an angry whine. Instinctively, we both ducked our heads.

"...anyway, he couldn't see me through the brush, but he must have heard me..."

I rolled to my left and gathered my knees under me, then pushed myself up so I was sitting on my heels. I quickly glanced at Jack. He was reloading the scattergun.

"...cause he's just standing there. So I stepped out in the open..."

I saw movement behind the roots of an overturned spruce. He was closer to the cleft.

'*If he gets back in there,*' I thought to myself, '*We'll have to wait him out.*'

I made a snap shot and peeled bark from the spruce. Bear Robe Man sprinted toward the cleft and disappeared inside before I could make a follow-up shot.

"...and that's what happened," said Yukon Jack as he finished his story.

I looked at Jack then realized I had not heard all he had said.

"What was that last part? The part where you stepped out from behind the willows or whatever?"

Jack started to turn to fire the shotgun.

"Forget about him," I said. "He's already made it back into the cleft."

Jack frowned and sat back against the rock.

"I said, I told him to throw up his hands, or some such, and he dropped his canteen and tried to bring his rifle up. I fired a slug an' missed. He got off a round that went through the brush. I decided to seek shelter, so I gave him the second barrel with double-aught buck and dove down behind this here boulder. That's when you showed up, and that's what happened."

As with most gunfights, it only lasted minutes but seemed like an eternity. Your life and that of your opponent hangs on split-second decisions that can never be taken back. Society, with the benefit of hindsight, will always judge you on those split-second decisions made in the heat of the moment.

"Sorry you had to face him alone," I said. "I should have stayed here and watched with you. Should have known he was going to get water before nightfall."

"Nonsense, young-un. They ain't no way you could've known for sure he was going to come out for water. Besides, you needed food in your belly, too."

Well, one positive came out of this confrontation. Bear Robe Man no longer had a canteen. '*He is going to be mighty thirsty come sun up.*'

I dug my watch out of my pocket, looked at it, and said, "The suns goin' ta set a little after ten. That gives us about an hour and forty-five minutes."

I clasped the watch shut and shoved it back into my pocket. Looking at Jack I said, "I figure he knows we can outlast him, so he's going to make his move after sunset. You sure he can't climb up out of that cleft?"

Jack looked at me, frowned, and said, "No, I ain't sure. Anything's possible I guess."

I turned my head and looked at the eastern wall of the canyon and the cleft where Bear Robe Man was holed up. I highly doubted he would try a stunt like that, and it was too late in the day to send Jack across the creek and up the other canyon wall to intercept him if he did.

Looking back at Jack I said, "We're just gonna have to watch that cleft through the twilight hours till sunup. If he doesn't try to make a break for it in the twilight, then I'm going in after him. It's time to get this over with."

CHAPTER 14

JACK AND I TOOK TURNS dozing and swatting mosquitoes next to the creek, as we watched the cleft in the eastern wall of the canyon.

The combined four hours of sunset and sunrise seemed to pass slowly as I deliberated on how to execute the plan. I figured working my way into the cleft to confront Bear Robe Man, would be kin to working my way through thick alder to find a wounded grizzly. Facing down a wounded grizzly, I had experience with. Shooting it out toe-to-toe with a desperate man, not so much. Once again, I found myself wishing I had brought my revolver for close-quarters work.

I looked at my watch. Five minutes after three. '*The sun will be up in about fifteen minutes.*'

I gently nudged Jack awake.

"Time to get after it," I said.

Jack grunted, rubbed his eyes, and looked around.

"Alright," he half whispered.

As we stretched the kinks out of our bodies and checked our gear, I asked Jack if he had heard anything during his watch.

"Nothing unusual. I heard some rock fall a time or two. But, again, that's nothing unusual in this canyon."

"Well, I'm just going to have to go in there and roust him out. Get this over with."

Ten minutes later, I took a dip of Copenhagen and replaced it in my pants pocket. I released the safety on my rifle and opened the bolt to make sure there was a cartridge in the chamber. I closed the bolt, left the safety off, cradled the rifle in the crook of my left arm, and turned to Jack.

"When we get to the other side of the creek, wait for me outside of the cleft. Don't stand in the mouth of it, neither. A bullet may come ricocheting out of the entrance and hit ya. If he gets by me, it'll be up to you to stop him."

"I got your back, young-un. Just keep your wits about ya, ya hear?" he said.

When we got to the cleft, I wiped my palms dry on my pant legs, looked at Jack, and tightened my grip on the rifle. Jack made eye contact with me and shook his head once.

"Lord, please be with me," I whispered.

I turned, raised my rifle to my shoulder in the high ready position, and headed into the cleft.

A few careful, slow steps, then the thought flitted through my mind and seared my brain like a branding iron. '*What will become of Corrine and our child if I lose?*' I shook my head trying to clear it. '*No time to think of that now.*'

A few more steps and all excess noise began to fade away. A couple more steps and a death-like silence engulfed me like water around a drowning swimmer. My pulse pounded in my temples, I fought for every breath. I felt myself losing control and I fought to regain it. And always, always the death-like stillness.

Two more steps.

Every nerve and every one of my five senses was raw and on edge. Up ahead I could see a mosquito resting on a pebble. I could smell the tangy-sweet aroma of *Hoppes* I had used to clean my rifle three days ago. Somewhere in the distance, I heard dust trickle down the rock wall.

By now, the cleft had narrowed, so that I could touch each wall with my hands outstretched. Up ahead, the passageway made a slight turn to the right.

I switched the rifle to the left-hand shooting position, and looking down the barrel, I half-stepped around the corner, inspecting each new area exposed by the half-step.

With that corner cleared, I could see the passageway made another slight turn, this time to my left. Switching my rifle to the right-hand shooting position, I repeated the process. However, this time, each new half-step view confirmed with the others I was coming to the end of the cleft.

'*Where is he?*' I asked myself. '*He has got to be hiding just around the corner*', I decided.

Two more careful, quiet half steps.

'*What should I do?*' I asked myself. '*He probably knows I'm here, waiting for me to stick my rifle barrel around the corner. If I do that, it will give my position away before he sees me. No, I'll jump around the corner, possibly surprising him, get the drop on him.*'

Summoning up my reserve energy, I crouched a little, and then sprang as far as I could past the curve, dropped to my knees in the sand, and rolled.

I brought my rifle up and yelled, "DON'T MOVE!"

Bear Robe Man was not there.

CHAPTER 15

A T FIRST, SHOCK SET IN at not finding what I had expected. Then rage. My hands shook from the adrenaline and anger that coursed through my veins. Bear Robe Man had outsmarted me and did exactly what I expected him not to do.

At this point, the cleft pinched out to nothing. Looking up, I could clearly see how a man could climb up out of here by pressing hands and feet against the opposing walls, and thus, working his way to the top.

I got to my feet, and, looking around his camp, I saw a snow drift still lingering in the cool shadows. The dusty top layer had been carefully scraped off, exposing the white clean snow beneath. A scooped-out depression in the clean snow had provided fresh water for Bear Robe Man.

The fire pit revealed nothing, except, perhaps that Bear Robe Man had nothing to eat. There were no indications of food scraps.

I made my way back out to the opening and told Jack what I had found.

"Well, young-un, now what are we gonna do?" he asked.

I thought a bit, then said, "First, we'll go back to camp and pack up. I'll take the cotton rope. Then I want you and Kitty to work your way up to the shelf. I'll climb up the cleft, like Bear Robe Man obviously did, then pull my pack and rifle up after me."

"Why don't ya come with us? It'll be easier gettin' to the top."

"Easier maybe, but it'll take longer. I want to be able to locate sign where he crawled out of this cleft. Maybe work out a direction of travel by the time you and Kitty get up there."

"Well, you're the boss," Jack said. "Just be careful and don't take any unnecessary chances. You end up breaking a leg or something, and I'm gonna just leave ya here."

I frowned and looked sideways at Jack, as he turned and headed for the creek and our camp on the other side.

After packing up our gear, I made my way back to the end of the cleft. I dropped my pack and tied one end of the rope to the shoulder straps. The rest of the rope I laid out in a figure eight and tied the other end around my waist with a bowline hitch so it would not tighten up around my waist. I hoped there was enough rope to let me reach the ledge.

With the rifle slung from my left shoulder to my right underarm, I looked up the narrow cleft and decided, '*If he can do it, I can, too.*'

So, with both hands and both feet forced against the opposing walls, I inched my way up. I did pretty well until four feet from the top. I ran out of rope and felt the fifty-pound tug of the backpack as I transferred my weight to my right foot to raise myself up a few more inches. The unexpected weight threw me off-balance and my right foot lost its purchase against the wall. Luckily, as it slid down a few inches, it caught another ledge and stopped my descent.

'*Whew...that was a close one*,' I thought to myself. '*Thank you, Lord.*'

I finally made it to the top and slowly peeked over the edge. The coast was clear. I squirmed myself up and over the edge, turned and sat up. I unslung my rifle from my shoulder and laid it to the side. Then, I pulled my pack up by the rope, then coiled the rope, and stashed it in the pack.

Looking around, I realized there was a smoky haze in the air. I could see the bench top land was covered with hard packed decomposed granite cobbles, stunted low-bush cranberry brush, and caribou moss. Along the ledge I was sitting on, I found bear hair that, evidently, had been scraped off the robe when

Bear Robe Man pulled himself up over the edge as I had just done. I also found blood stains smeared on the edge of the rock ledge.

'*Was Bear Robe Man wounded in the shootout*,' I wondered? '*Or did he just injure himself while climbing up?*' If he was wounded, it would definitely slow him down a little. Other than that, there was nothing else. No sign anywhere that he or anything else had been here.

Again, self-doubt crept into my brain as I searched. A little voice in my head said, '*You're going to lose this guy like the last man you tracked.*' Then I got mad. '*NO! Stop thinkin' like that. That's stinkin' thinkin. The sign is here somewhere. Find it!*'

A half-hour later, I was still looking for sign of Bear Robe Man's passage. I had cut half circles around the cleft opening from the cliff edge upstream, to the cliff edge downstream, a hundred yards out. I had studied pert-near every stone in my paths to see if any had been over-turned or dislodged. I had checked for bruised, crushed, or broken vegetation. I had even kept an eye out for strands of bear hair, the reliable 'tell'. All to no avail.

I was thoroughly disgusted with myself. There had to be sign here somewhere. Nothing, whether it be man or beast moves through this world without leaving some evidence behind of its passage. The trick is to find that evidence and interpret, or read, it properly.

To add insult to injury, the faint smell of smoke made me realize the smoky haze from a distant forest fire was increasing. It diffused the sunlight. There were no shadows. Shadows are a trackers friend. The longer the shadows, the better. A good tracker always tries to keep the tracks he follows between him and the sun. In this way, the sun will cast a shadow from the edge of the print, into the print, that is easily seen. If the sun is behind you, the shadow is not nearly as distinct. However, on this hard-packed, decomposed granite, if there were any prints, they would be very shallow or nonexistent.

'*Well, you let another one get away,*' said the voice inside my head.

Looking around, I saw Yukon Jack and Kitty making their way along the rimrocks in my direction. I turned and started walking to meet them when something on the ground made me stop. I was not sure what it was I had seen that caught my attention. Looking closer, I could see what possibly could be a slight depression. It did not look like anything important, but my brain would not let it go. I decided to tie a piece of my bandana to the brush next to the spot so I could come back to it later, then I left to meet Jack.

I met Jack and Kitty back at the cleft and showed him what I had found. Then I explained my dilemma about the absence of any sign, or, at least, my inability to find it.

I picked up a hand full of pebbles and absentmindedly tossed one down into the cleft.

"Jack, I'm washed up, I guess. I told the Marshal it had been a long time since I had done any man tracking, and that I no longer felt competent enough to do so. I let my last target get away..." I tossed another pebble into the cleft, "...and now it looks like I've lost another one," I said as I tossed another pebble.

"Nonsense young-un. Why I've seen ya do things within the last three days that most men could never do. I've looked at the same spot of ground you were looking at and wondered, 'What does he see that I don't?' Then when ya pointed it out, it was plain as day. Big guy, ya got a gift. Shure, it's hard tracking right now, but it's no reflection on you. Ya need to relax and trust your instincts."

"In other words, stop feeling sorry for myself?" I asked as I tossed another pebble into the cleft and watched it fall.

"Exactly. Look, if worse comes to worst, we know or at least have a pretty good idea, he's headed to Circle City. I'm for high-tailin' it there and lookin' for 'im. Maybe catch 'im afore he boards a stern-wheeler for Dawson."

Jack was right. We could just head to Circle City, but I had something to prove, if only to myself.

"Jack, we know he's here. The last known sign is right there on the edge of that cleft in the rock wall. We're only a couple of hours behind him, and I think he's hurt. I'd rather stick with a sure thing then go traipsin' to Circle after a possibility."

Jack looked at me for three or four seconds, shook his head once and said, "Okay. Let's get after 'im."

CHAPTER 16

BACK AT THE SPOT WHERE I had tied the piece of bandana to mark the possible print, I showed Jack the slight indentation on the ground and asked him what he thought of it. He studied it from every angle then sat down cross-legged in front of me and with the possible track between us.

"I don't know," Jack said while scratching his beard. "Seems to be a slight ridge along one side, but I can't tell. With this flat light, I just can't make out any detail."

I looked around at the smoky sky in disgust and noticed a bright spot where the sun was trying to shine through occasionally.

"Wish we had some way of concentrating light," I said half out loud.

"Well...I got a mirror," Jack said. "Would that help?"

I looked back at him. "You packed along a mirror? What for?"

"Well, ya never know. I gotta look good for the ladies if'n we should meet some," Jack said with a serious look on his face.

I did not know how to respond to that. I just looked at him for a couple of seconds then laughed.

"What're you laughing at? It could happen!"

"Alright," I said. "Dig it out. I got an idea."

As Jack rummaged through his pack for the mirror, I untied my wool blanket from my pack.

"Fixin' to spend the night, are ya?" Jack asked.

I looked up at Jack. "No. I'm going to pull this blanket over my head and that possible print to block out most of the light. Then, I want you to get down low to the ground and reflect as much light from the bright spot where the sun is, under the blanket and across that possible print. If it works, it should cast a good shadow and illuminate the outline of the print."

It took a little maneuvering on both our parts, but suddenly, the print stood out clearly. It was the heel of a boot, and the only person in this area beside Jack and I was Bear Robe Man.

That made me smile.

"Got him, Jack," I said as I threw off the blanket.

I reached for the measuring stick and pulled it out of my pack. Next, I laid the bottom notch on the back edge of the depression of the heel strike and then swung the front end in a slow arc, looking at the tip for indications of another heel strike.

Suddenly, there it was. Two or three broken stems of caribou moss, barely discernible, but there, none-the-less. Using the same procedure, I found a broken twig lying across a stone that had been pushed down into the hard-packed soil.

Looking up and ahead, in line with the three tracks, I could see Bear Robe Man's line of travel was north along this bench. To the right, the land rose up to the ridge.

"Jack, I'm going to climb up there and glass as much country ahead as I can. Maybe I can spot him. I want you to hike along this bench a-ways. Maybe flush him out if he's hiding in that thicker brush-up yonder. Keep an eye on me from time-to-time, though. If I spot him, I'll let you know."

I reached the ridge top about twenty minutes later, sat my pack down, and quickly scanned the bench I had left below.

I realized that the bench swung east up a little draw, then petered out into a small valley further east, and on the opposite side of the ridge I stood on.

Many caribou trails converged from the

creek bottom where we had been, onto the bench, then into that valley.

I dug out my binoculars, found a comfortable seat, rested my elbows against my knees, and began to study the terrain.

Judging by the torn-up trails, it was obvious some caribou had been through here recently, probably the pregnant cows heading somewhere to their calving grounds. The main herd, the yearlings, dry cows, and bulls, would be along shortly, I figured. All sign of Bear Robe Man's passing will be obliterated if he falls in with the herd.

As I swung my binoculars up the small valley, movement caught my eye. Looking closer, I counted seven cows trotting up one of the trails. Something had spooked them. Wolves trailing them, maybe?

Looking down the small valley, a black spot, moving along one of the trails almost confirmed my suspicion. However, I looked again.

It was Bear Robe Man.

CHAPTER 17

I REALIZED I WAS SKY-LINED FROM Bear Robe Man's perspective, so I hunkered down and eased back a few steps. Looking back at Jack, I could see Kitty just ahead of him. I gave a short, loud whistle and she stopped and looked in my direction. Jack evidently noticed her and turned toward me. Taking what was left of my red bandanna, I waved it over my head to get his attention. Seconds later, he turned and began to climb toward me.

Turning, I crawled back to the ridge-line and watched Bear Robe Man's progress through the binoculars.

Closer to me, and heading toward Bear Robe Man, I saw a few more caribou filing along the myriad of game trails, heading up country, following the cows. It was the leading edge of the main herd. Soon, any sign of Bear Robe Man's passing would be gone. Fortunately, I did not need to worry about that much, because I could clearly see him and his intended destination: a big outcropping of granite on the upper end of the valley. It appeared all the game trails converged to the right of that outcropping and crossed over the ridge.

Bear Robe Man had not made as much distance as I figured he might have. A small rivulet of water, perhaps two feet wide meandered down the valley floor. I observed Bear Robe Man stop from time to time to drink from it. I believe the pure protein diet and the possible wound with his loss of blood, was slowing him down and making him thirsty.

Jack suddenly dropped down beside me and startled me.

"Easy, big guy. It's just us," he said as he glanced at me. "Whatcha got?"

I handed Jack the binoculars.

"He's down there following those caribou up country. The trails seem to swing a little south and converge on this ridge we're on, a couple miles ahead, by that granite outcrop. I'm thinking if we stay just below the ridgeline on the south side, and hightail it ahead, we can intercept him when he reaches the ridge. Of course, we're going to have to beat the main herd and cross their trail, or we may lose him until the heard goes by. There's at least three thousand head in that bunch."

Jack lowered the binoculars, rubbed his chin whiskers, and said, "Sounds like a plan."

We crouched, trying to keep our profile as low as possible, and worked our way to the south-facing slope, then turned east. From there, I began to jog and Jack brought up the rear as fast as he could go.

Twenty minutes later, I got a stitch in my side and had to slow down to a walk. I decided it might be a good time to check our progress. Laying my pack down, I crouched and made my way to the ridge-line. On hands and knees, I cautiously peered over the top into the valley below.

I was closer to Bear Robe Man, but he was still ahead of me, working his way up the slope toward the granite tor. Looking down the valley, I could see the main herd coming fast. It was going to be questionable who got to the crossing first. Bear Robe Man, the caribou, or me.

I crab-walked backward until I could not see Bear Robe Man, then got to my feet and made it back to my pack. I took a couple of slugs of water from the canteen and replaced it in my pack. The brief rest and the cool water seemed to help alleviate the stitch in my side.

Donning my pack, and with rifle in hand, again I jogged east along the south slope just under the ridge-line. Soon, I could tell I was getting close to the caribou migration trail from the position of the granite outcrop ahead of me. The one Bear Robe Man was headed to.

All the game trails converged at this spot and crossed over to the south-facing slope. In a few minutes, three thousand head of caribou would be pouring over the ridge between Bear Robe Man and me, to the valley on the south side. I had to get to him first before the caribou got here, or I would be cut off from him.

Throwing my pack to the side, I unslung my rifle and eased up to the ridge-line to locate Bear Robe Man. As I reached the top, I became aware of a low rumbling sound. Looking to my left, down the valley toward the sound, I could see the herd, a couple hundred yards away, all in a trot, anxious to reach the top.

Looking to the right, another couple of hundred yards, Bear Robe Man was trying to climb up out of their way to the granite outcrop. If I could beat the herd before they got to the ridge-line, I could have him trapped between the caribou, the granite tor, and myself.

At a dead run, I headed toward the migration trail. Five yards from the trail, I heard an angry buzz zip past my head, and then the report of a rifle. Instantly I knew Bear Robe Man had spotted me, and I dove toward the south-facing slope and rolled. Another round spat gravel, dirt, and bullet fragments in my face and stung my eyes.

By now, the low rumble was louder, and I could hear the low, pig-like grunts the caribou make and the clicking of cloven hooves on stone. I thought I had lost the race.

Looking up, through bleary, watery eyes, I saw the first five or six caribou appear over the ridge. Suddenly, they stopped, staring wide-eyed at me, evidently not knowing if I was a threat or not. The relentless push of the rest of the herd from behind compelled them to continue or be trampled. Giving an alarmed grunt, they leaped to either side of me and continued over the ridge.

I had a choice: either stay here and get trampled or try to make it to the safety of the rock. I chose the latter. I squeezed my eyes shut and tried to clear my vision, and then, gathering my feet under me, and with my rifle in hand, I sprang into a dead run for the granite outcrop, dodging caribou as more and more of them poured over the ridge.

Reaching the safety of the rock face, I placed my back against it, dug out my bandanna, and tried to wipe the dust and rock fragments from my watering eyes. I noticed blood streaks on the bandanna. Wide-eyed caribou, hemmed in by me and the rock wall on one side, and the relentless push from the rest of the herd on the other side and behind, flowed by so close I could have reached out and touched them.

Startled grunts of alarm from those near me, mixed with the low pig-like grunts of the rest of the herd, blended with the clicking of antlers and hooves as they churned up the alpine tundra and stones in their determined push to reach the other side.

Keeping my back to the granite wall, I sidestepped my way between it and the herd to relative safety on the south side of the outcrop.

Taking a moment to catch my breath, and wipe my eyes again, I quickly thought about the situation.

My last glimpse of Bear Robe Man indicated he was working his way to the east side of the outcrop.

'*It is possible he thinks I was cut off or trampled by the herd and he is heading on east to Circle City. On the other hand, it is also possible he is curious and wants to know exactly where I am; in which case, he would probably climb up on this outcrop to get a better view. Jack is still making his way along the ridge on the other side of the herd, and is of no help to me. I have to locate Bear Robe Man.*'

I replaced the bandana then unlocked the rifle bolt and opened it just enough to visually make sure there was a round in the chamber. Then I closed the bolt and locked it down, checked the safety, and raised the rifle to my shoulder at low ready.

My eyes continued to water and I squeezed them shut and shook my head to get rid of the tears. I raised the rifle to high ready, turned, took two steps away from the rock, and checked the skyline of the towering outcrop above me.

All clear.

At low ready, I worked my way around the base of the outcrop until I had a dimmed view of the eastbound ridge. Again, I squeezed my eyes shut to clear the tears, then looked again.

Bear Robe Man was not there.

I began to turn.

"Hold it right there... unless you want to meet your maker."

CHAPTER 18

"RAISE YOUR HANDS AND FACE me," the voice behind me said. "I want to see the man that's been doggin' me these last few days afore I kill ya."

I did as he said, holding my rifle in my right hand.

Bear Robe Man was standing on a ledge of the outcrop about six feet up, his rifle pointed at my chest. I could see what looked like a blood stain on his upper left shoulder.

"Toss that shootin' iron, easy like."

Several boulders of granite had tumbled off the outcrop in years past, and I tossed the rifle toward a large one, in such a way that it would land butt first on the ground. I did not want to take the chance of it landing muzzle first and plug up with dirt. I figured if I got the chance, I could dive toward that boulder for cover and have a fair chance at retrieving my rifle. I just hoped Bear Robe Man hadn't picked up on it.

Looking me up and down, he asked, "You the one that was at my cabin the other day? You a lawman, or something?"

"Temporarily. Marshal Sullivan asked me to track ya down and bring ya in for questioning about those miners with missing teeth. I also got questions about Henry Cravats. I guess now's as good a time as any to tell ya you're under arrest."

Bear Robe Man's brow furrowed, then a smile crossed his face. Laughter erupted as he threw back his head then looked at me and said, "Mister, either you're a fool or you're the bravest man I ever met."

I just shrugged my shoulders once, in answer and squeezed my eyes shut, still trying to clear my vision.

"You know, I could have killed ya a time or two."

Again, I just nodded my head once, then said, "Yeah, I realized that when I found where you had watched me. Why didn't ya?"

He shrugged.

"Curiosity. I never knew a white man who could track like that. Except once, back in Montana. You remind me a lot of that feller, and I wanted to see just how good you were."

Montana. The parts of the puzzle were coming together in my mind. I was sure this was the same man I had tracked all those years ago and lost; the one who later killed the farmer, his wife, and kids. Rage began to boil inside and tied my guts in knots, and the lust for revenge had awakened.

I decided to try to keep him talking, hoping to give more time to the herd of caribou still rumbling over the ridge on the other side of this outcrop to my left.

Jack was over there, somewhere, trying to get through.

By now, my eyes were not stinging or watering as bad.

"You must be Judas Cain!" I said in a lowered voice through clenched jaws.

I knew that got his attention. I could see his expression change a little.

He started to say something, hesitated a couple of seconds, and then asked, "How you know that?"

"I know plenty about you," I said as I slowly lowered my hands. I was getting tired of holding them up.

"You don't know nuthin' about me. Get them hands back up."

I raised my hands.

I decided to push it a little more.

"I know your father was a half-breed Comanche called Tosahwi Cain, also known as White Knife, born of a white captive slave.

I also know your mother was a white captive of the Northern Cheyenne," I said.

Then I paused to let that sink in.

He raised his cheek up off the rifle stock, lowered the muzzle just a bit and said, "True enough. How you know so much about me?"

"Anytime I go huntin', whether it be man or beast, I make it my business to learn all I can about the prey," I said as I slowly began to lower my hands again.

I could almost see the wheels turning in his brain as he chewed on that, and I knew in a second or two, he would realize I was lowering my hands.

Cain suddenly raised the muzzle of his rifle and planted his cheek on the stock.

I continued talking.

"I also know you worked for a horse thief called Dutch Henry out of Valley County Montana back in 1901."

"So, what's your point?"

By now, the low rumble of caribou hooves had died down a little, and I knew the end of the herd was close to crossing the ridge.

If Yukon Jack was waiting just on the other side, he could soon come walking around this big rock, stumble into this mess, and get himself or me shot.

"I'm the one who tracked you into the

Upper Missouri Brakes."

Again, he raised his cheek from the butt-stock and looked closely at me. Then a thin smile crossed his face.

"So you're the one. You dogged me pretty good. Killed my horse trying to shake you. Finally did too, after I was on foot."

I had him talking now, remembering.

I shook my head. "Yep. Lost ya in the rim rocks."

He lowered his rifle and cradled it in the crook of his left arm.

I took two steps to my right, casual like, and leaned up against the large boulder. I was hoping my body mostly hid the rifle lying on the ground behind me.

His rifle came up as I moved, but he did not say anything.

I raised my hands and said, "Easy, easy. Just need to rest my back a little."

I pointed to my pants pocket and asked, "You mind?"

He tossed his head once and lowered the rifle a little. I took out my Copenhagen, took a dip, and then offered him some.

He shook his head. "No thanks. I can do without it."

"Yeah I need to quit this stuff myself," I said as I put it away.

I kept stalling, trying to get Cain to settle down some more—get him to lower his guard. I needed to be on a more equal footing with him.

Call it professional pride, but I needed to know one thing…"So, how did I lose ya in the rim rocks back then?"

He smiled and then did something totally unexpected. He sat down on the ledge, then slid off it and landed on his feet no more than eight feet in front of me. All the while keeping his rifle trained on me.

'*That's more like it*', I thought to myself as I shifted my weight from the boulder I was leaning on, to the balls of my feet. My hands came up defensively, chest high, and I turned slightly to a forty-five-degree angle from him. I was not sure of his intentions.

"You didn't lose me," he growled. "You walked twice past me so close I could have spit on you. It was just dumb luck you didn't see me squeezed into that crack in the wall on the ledge above the river. Anyway," he continued with a slight grin, "after you went by the second time, I just dove off the ledge into the Missouri. Then, I floated downstream with some driftwood for a couple or three days."

By now, his rifle had lowered somewhat, evidently from fatigue in his arms. His eyes momentarily drifted to my left, toward the last few caribou filing over the ridge top. I briefly wondered if he had suddenly remembered Yukon Jack was over there, somewhere. I had to get his mind back on me.

"So, that's when you killed the farmer and stole a couple of horses?" I asked as I took a small step toward him.

His eyes met mine and I saw his jaw muscles tighten a little. "Who says that was me?"

"The bloody, turned-in left footprint you left on the farmhouse floor. That's who."

He glanced down at his left foot. I took a small step forward. He looked back at me.

"Why did you kill his wife?" I asked.

"The ungrateful wench pulled a shotgun on me. All I was tryin' to do was be friendly like."

"Why did you kill the little boy and girl? They were just kids!"

The grin disappeared. He gave me a quick look up and down as if sizing me up. "Why you so interested in that farmer anyway?"

I was seething inside. Hate and contempt for this man, along with feelings of guilt because I did not catch him years ago, bubbled to the surface and I began to shake. I wanted revenge.

Through clenched teeth I said, "The farmer was my brother-in-law. His wife was my sister."

"Aw..." he said as he slowly nodded his head up and down, studying me for a few seconds. Then, he shrugged his shoulders, grinned.

"The kids? Well, I couldn't afford to leave no witnesses."

CHAPTER 19

I HAD SEEN THE HANDIWORK OF Judas Cain on Henry Cravats, and I knew I was in for the fight of my life. Never the less, it was my duty to attempt to take him into custody, and this was as good a time as any.

I squeezed my eyes shut to force out the excess tearing, spun on the ball of my left foot and the toe of my right while rolling my shoulders, and pulped his lips with a straight right-hand punch.

Cain dropped his rifle, staggered backward a step, and slammed into the ledge he had been standing on.

I stepped in and followed with a quick left to the cheekbone and blood showed.

Stepping backward, I drug my shirtsleeve across my eyes to clear them.

Then a roar escaped Cain's lungs and I knew he had recovered from the shock and I had awakened the beast within.

He charged then and threw a roundhouse punch that caught me on the chin that shook me to my toes.

I staggered, fell sideways against the boulder, and then rolled to my back to face Cain.

He came at me, grabbed my shirt collar with both hands, and jerked a knee up toward my groin.

I twisted to the left and caught his knee a glancing blow on my thigh.

The follow-through landed his knee against the boulder. He groaned and loosened his grip on my collar.

Breaking his hold, I continued to spin to the left and landed a right to his cheekbone, splitting it open even more.

Cain staggered a couple of steps sideways. Then, another roaring yell escaped his lips as he turned and charged.

I did not retreat but stepped into him with a right to the solar plexus and a left to the ribs.

Cain gasped, trying to catch his wind and I backed up a step to give myself room—my own lungs screaming for air.

Cain rushed me again.

Toe-to-toe we stood, slugging it out, with each blow sounding like a rock hitting mud.

I felt blood run down my face from a cut above my eye and a smashed nose, and my head buzzed from the impacts of Cain's ponderous fists.

Lights flashed as a fist landed on my jaw.

I felt my knees turn to jelly, and then the ground came up hard and fast to meet me as I fell.

Somewhere, there was an explosion, and then all was still.

In a dream-like state, I felt as if I was floating gently with clouds in a cerulean blue sky, and I was peaceful and content.

Then I remembered the fight and wondered if I had died, and was now in heaven.

Gradually, I became aware of puffs of air drifting over my skin, soft and gentle, like butterfly wings. I turned, opened my eyes, and saw Kitty lying next to me, panting doggy breath in my face. The peaceful blue skies of my subconscience gave way to the ugly smoky haze of reality and I tried to sit up.

Then, a pounding exploded in my head and I suddenly had to throw up. With each retching convulsion, the pounding got worse. Finally, the retching stopped.

"You were out for a while, Young-un. Musta had a concussion."

I turned my head toward the voice and saw Yukon Jack sitting with his back against a boulder, poking his diamond willow walking stick at a campfire.

"Where's Cain?" I asked in a raspy voice. My jaw hurt when I spoke and I reached up and felt it, working it back and forth. It did not feel like it was broken.

"Who?"

I cleared my throat, and then repeated, "Cain...Bear Robe Man."

Jack tossed his head to his left and said, "He's over yonder."

I tried to get up, but the pounding in my head made me sick again.

"Lay back down young-un. He ain't goin' nowhere soon."

I looked up at Jack, wiped my mouth with my shirtsleeve, and asked, "What do you mean by that?"

"He's dead."

I continued to look at Jack as the realization that it was all over, flooded my brain.

"You're lucky I got here when I did. I came around the corner of that outcrop just in time to see you hit the ground. Bear Robe Man pulled a Bowie out from under his robe and stood over you. I debated whether to shoot you or him. I decided I liked you better," he said as a grin crossed his face.

I tried to smile too, but it hurt too much. I laid back down and gingerly felt of my swollen face. Evidently, Jack had bandaged the cut above my eye. Under the bandage, I could feel a goose egg.

"Every inch of me hurts," I said.

"I got some headache powder in my pack, but you should probably try to eat something first."

Jack dug through Kitty's pack and pulled out a tin of peaches. This, he opened with his knife, folded back the lid into sort of a handle, then handed it to me. I slowly pushed myself into a sitting position without throwing up again, took the can, and sipped some of the juice.

"Eat the peaches first," he said, as he handed me a forked stick. "Then we'll mix the headache powder in with the juice. It'll go down better."

Twenty minutes later, the pounding in my head had dulled some, and I was able to keep the peaches down. During that time, I had given Jack some paper and a pencil and told him to write everything down while it was still fresh in his mind.

I read it and laid it aside.

"One thing still bothers me," I said. "I don't know for sure if he's the one that killed those miners for their gold fillings or not."

CHAPTER 20

"WHERE YA HEADED?" JACK ASKED as I stood a little unsteadily on my feet. My head still swam some from the punches I had taken.

"I need to see the body and inventory his personal effects," I answered as I made my way in the direction Jack had indicated earlier.

"I'll go with ya."

Next to the boulder where I had tossed my rifle earlier, the body of Judas Cain lay in a heap on his stomach.

Rolling him over and straightening out his limbs took some effort. Rigor mortis had set in. His death mask revealed a hideous toothy grin, as if, even in death, he was not going to make things easy.

Jack and I began going through his pack and pockets, laying everything aside to be recorded in my ledger.

We found:

- One pocket compass
- One knife (Bowie style)
- An assortment of fish hooks and line
- One dead squirrel
- Fifteen white pills wrapped in paper
- One hatchet
- Eleven teeth with gold fillings in a poke that hung around his neck
- One Krag .$^{30}/_{40}$ rifle with eighteen rounds of ammunition
- One large fire blackened tin can with a bailing wire handle
- One bundle of matches dipped in paraffin

"Anything else?" I asked as I scribbled the last entry in the ledger.

"Other than what he's wearing and the pack, that's it. I guess those teeth with the gold fillings, pretty much answered your question about whether he's the right person or not, huh?"

"It's pretty convincing circumstantial evidence alright," I answered.

I put the ledger and pencil in my pack and then sighed heavily as I looked at the body, thinking about the task ahead.

Looking over at Jack, I saw he was studying me.

"Let's worry about him tomorrow," he said.

"You need to rest some and get some food in your belly."

I didn't argue with him. I was stiff and sore from the fight, and the pounding in my head had returned.

* * *

That night, not much was spoken, each lost in our own thoughts.

It was but eight months ago, I was foot-loose trying to make my own way as a trapper and meat hunter with a gnawing hunger deep inside for something I did not want to admit.

Then the good Lord crossed my path with Corrine's and I had to accept the fact that I was not complete. I needed the love of a good woman to make me whole. '*And now, I find she's going to give me a child. Aw… and Jack.*' He was there, too, to teach me a few things. Things like, never give up, and always try to make the best of a bad situation. A little humor never hurts.

I looked across the campfire at the old sourdough. He was staring at the fire, poking his diamond willow walking stick at the embers.

"Jack Susan Farley." I watched him closely as I spoke his full name.

Jack stiffened, his eyes grew wide and he spun his head to look at me so fast, I thought his neck might snap. It made me smile.

"How'd you know my middle name?"

"I got ways," I said, as I continued to smile at him.

"Well, don't go spreadin' it around," he said as he looked back at the fire. "I hate that name...well, for a guy anyway." He poked at the fire again.

"If we have a boy, I'd like to name him after you."

Jack stopped poking the fire and sat still for a moment. Then he reached up and brushed something off his cheek.

"I'd be right proud," he said. "Just don't call him Susan."

I laughed and said, "I won't."

Still poking at the fire, Jack said, "My mother gave me that middle name. She wanted a girl."

"Well, if we have a girl, can I name her Susan?"

Jack looked back at me, smiled and said, "Yeah, I reckon that'll be okay."

We sat silent, once again, watching the fire burn as my thoughts turned back to Judas Cain.

"It's kinda strange," I said, "after all these years and miles, how my path converged with my sister's killer, the one who escaped me all those years ago. It's like...it's like the good

Lord gave me a second chance to track Cain down. But, if that's the case, why did he let him almost kill me? If it hadn't been for you, he would have."

A slight smile crossed Jack's face. "As Robert Service once wrote, 'There are strange things done 'neath the midnight sun...'. I think, if you had had the upper hand, you would have killed Cain, and it would have been revenge, not justice. 'Vengeance is mine; I will repay, saith the Lord'.

"Cain is now getting his just reward. Ungodly men like him don't understand what's important in life. Things like putting God first, a good wife and young-uns scurrying about your feet, a snug cabin, meat in the cache and a good lead dog that'll never steer ya wrong. I can't prove it, but I think Wyatt Earp found that out when he ended up in Nome a few years ago."

A few moments passed as we again stared into the fire. I began to feel as if there was something on his mind he wanted to say. I decided not to pry. He would say it in his own good time.

"You're goin'a have a hard time getting' him back to Fairbanks," he suddenly said.

He must have been reading my mind.

"Yeah, I was just thinking about that. I figure we can build some sort of travois and, with you, me and Kitty pulling, maybe we can get him back to the placer mine, and from there down the mail trail to Chatanika somehow."

Jack looked away from me as if studying the countryside for a few seconds, then looked back at me.

"I been meanin' to talk to you about that. I ain't going back to Fairbanks."

"What?" I asked as I looked at him trying to comprehend what he was saying.

Jack looked down at his feet, swallowed hard and said, "I been trying to figure a way of tellin' ya this for the last few days. Me and Kitty's headin' back to the Klondike. We may stop off at Fortymile and check out the diggin's there."

I quickly thought back over the last few days and realized that was why he had been in a sour mood a few times and why he wanted to just head to Circle City to pick up Cain's trail there.

"So that's why you've been in a surly mood, huh?"

Jack looked all around except at me.

"Yeah, I apologize about that. I guess I was just tryin' to make the break easier when it came." Then his eyes met mine and he said, "It ain't workin'."

"Why you wantin' to leave?"

"Young-un, you don't need me around no

more. You got a good woman and a son on the way to be your partners. Leastwise I'm bettin' it's a son. Besides, you saved my life last year, and now...," he tossed his head toward Judas Cain, "...I reckon I just saved your-un. I figure we're even."

I did not know what to say. I dropped my head, looked about my feet, trying to comprehend what was happening. Then, I looked back unto his face. His jaws tightened and he looked away.

* * *

The next morning, Jack and I carried Judas Cain's body to the foot of the granite tor and then covered him over with rocks a good four feet deep. It might have been a bit unorthodox, but I was not about to pack his two-hundred-and-thirty-some pound carcass back to Fairbanks by myself.

With that chore finished, I turned to Jack.

"You sure about your decision to head back to the Klondike?"

He looked at me, smiled briefly, nodded his head once and said, "Yeah, there's a lady there I'd like to see."

"Alright," I said. "Well, if that's the lay of it, I wish ya luck, old friend. Corrine's going to miss you. You know you're like a grandfather to her?"

Jack looked away from me, his eyes scanning the horizon.

"Yeah, and she's like the daughter I never had." Then, looking back at me, "But she has a good man in you. I know you'll take care of her, cause if'n ya don't, I'll come back and kick your butt."

"You can try."

Jack looked away, coughed, then spat.

"Well..., at least I'll give ya a good cuff upside the head," he said as he looked back at me. Then he smiled.

* * *

ABOUT THE AUTHOR

RUSSELL M. CHACE IS THE author of the Alaska historical fiction novel *From Out of The Loneliness*. As a teenager and young adult, he learned much of what he writes, along the traplines and rivers he traveled by snowshoe, dog team and snow machine. It was during those years he wrote multiple articles for Alaska Magazine, Fishing and Hunting News, Voice of the Trapper and the Alaska trapper.

After moving to Colorado with his wife and two boys, Russell earned a degree in Criminal Justice and worked for the Colorado Department of Corrections for over twenty-two years. During that time, he was a member of the Emergency Response Team and the Escape Team, tracking escaped inmates in urban and suburban environments.

Russell is now retired and currently hard at work on his newest Alaska historical fiction novel. When not writing, he can be found fly-fishing, hunting, or prospecting the Arkansas River in the Rocky Mountains.